Emmabella's Easter Alphabet

E.E. Murray

Book B

By the same author

Emmabella's Christmas Alphabet
Book A

Emmabella's Birthday Alphabet
Book C

ISBN 1-980-47151-7

For Lucy

Contents

Introduction

This is the story of my Easter…

…And what an Easter it was. I suffered the greatest humiliation of my life, our holiday in the Lake District was a complete washout and I somehow found myself on top of a mountain with UNCLE DOUGIE.

I'm still trying to lead a neatly ordered and arranged life but nothing ever seems to work out the way I think it will. Whenever it seems that I have everything as I like it, some unforeseen thing will happen to knock everything off course. I have no idea why.

I don't know anybody else who tries to lead a neatly ordered and arranged life. My family and friends all seem to lead completely disorganised lives and they seem quite happy. Perhaps that's what I should try to do.

More than anything, though, I'm going to try to follow Nana Grundy's wise words. Nana Grundy is very fond of saying, 'Be careful what you wish for,' which means that what you wish for might not be what you want or need. Just before Easter, my wish was to be famous (famous in my small home town, at least) and as you are about to discover, it didn't go entirely to plan.

Anyway, my life might be a never-ending series of bewildering events but the way I tell my story is going to be organised; *this* is definitely going to be neatly ordered and arranged. And since the most neatly ordered and arranged thing in the entire universe is the alphabet (I think) I will tell you about my Easter logically: all the way from A to Z.

Here, then, is my Easter alphabet or, as Nana Grundy might say, 'Let's away!'

A is for Arrived

We arrived on the banks of Derwentwater in the Lake District on Good Friday morning. On the journey over, Dad asked us how many lakes there are in the Lake District. I said ninety-eight and Dad said 'Wrong.' Finn, my brother, said 'One' and Dad said, 'Well done, Finn.' How does Finn know these things? According to Dad (the old clever clogs), Bassenthwaite Lake is the only lake in the Lake District with the word 'lake' in its name so Bassenthwaite Lake is the only *actual* lake. There are lots of other lakes (not as many as ninety-eight, I later discovered) but these are all called 'meres' or 'waters'. So we were going to stay next to Derwentwater, which is *a* lake but not *the* lake.

In the car on the way to the Lake District, Mum and Dad were in the front and Finn and I were in the back. Mum and Dad were talking to each other (boring grown-up stuff – confirming that they'd locked the front door and not forgotten anything, that sort of thing) and Finn was reading a book called *The Art of War*.

Finn is lucky – he can read in a moving car. I can't – it always makes me car sick. If I even read so much as a line of text in a moving car I turn green and we have to pull over so I can throw up by the side of the road. I would have been about five-years-old when this started (probably around the time that I began to read properly) and since then, and because Dad hadn't managed to find anywhere to pull off the road in time, I've been banned from reading in the car. When I turned seven, I wondered if I might have grown out of this problem so I tried again. Luckily, Dad managed to find a lay-by in time and it was, again, 'recycled carrot soup time' as he calls it. When I was eight I thought I *must* have grown out of it and tried again. I hadn't grown out of it. Now I'm ten I'm old enough to know that I will have this problem for the rest of my life.

So I sat in the back of the car with no book for company and no conversation to share and stared out of the window as the dry stone walls and hills swept by. I drifted off and thought about all the things that had happened since Christmas.

Dad spent all of January and half of February hobbling around on crutches after breaking his ankle by crashing through my bedroom ceiling from the attic on to my bedroom floor on Christmas Eve. He never really got used to the crutches.

By the time the plaster was removed from his leg on February 14th (St Valentine's Day, about which more later) it was covered in various messages written with a marker pen by friends and family. Here's a sample of what was written:

Mum wrote: 'Just as good on one leg as two!' (What did *that* mean?).

Finn wrote: 'The path of the righteous man is beset on all sides by the inequities of the selfish and the tyranny of evil men.' (No? Me neither).

I wrote a little poem:

> 'Here's a message from Emmabella
> To Dad, a poor unfortunate fella!
> Your ankle's broke but don't be blue,
> Just be glad you didn't break two!'

(It was the best I could come up with at the time).

Auntie Maisie (Mum's sister) wrote: 'Save the planet and save the Library!'

Uncle Dougie (Maisie's husband) wrote: 'Don't let the b******s grind you down!' (I have used asterisks to save you from having to read what potty-mouthed Uncle Dougie actually wrote).

Nana Grundy (Mum's mum) wrote: 'Harvey got plastered at Christmas!'

Grandpa Grundy (Mum's dad) drew a cartoon of a bald man looking over the top of a wall (apparently he's called a 'Chad'. I had no idea why) and wrote underneath: 'Wot? No ankle!?' I didn't know what this meant either.

Mr Oddy, one of our next-door neighbours, wrote: 'Get well soon'. This was quite original considering what had already been written.

Over the six weeks that he wore it, I think Dad got quite attached to his cast. Obviously, he was attached to it (or, rather, it was attached to him) but he grew quite fond of it in a sentimental way, too. When he went back to the hospital to have it removed he asked if he could keep it. The two halves of the cast are now in the attic (appropriately since it was that attic that started all this off), never to be seen again, probably.

The attic floor, by the way, is now properly boarded out to stop Dad from ever falling through it again. It was done by the same man who re-plastered all our walls last year (The Man Who Knew What He Was Doing according to Mum) after Dad had wrecked the walls when he was taking all the old horrible woodchip wallpaper off them. The Man Who Knew What He Was Doing also repaired my bedroom ceiling and re-plastered it. Over the last few weeks, as the plaster has dried, my ceiling has changed colour from a deep brown to a nice light salmon pink. I quite like it, although I'm not quite so keen on the strange fishy smell coming from it.

In the first week of January, I started at Mr Coe's creative writing classes. Mr Coe is a local writer who believes that children should be taught to write well and that's why he runs a small writing class for ten and eleven-year-olds.

In one of the lessons, he told us that he went to a Grammar School where good grammar was drilled into him. Now, as a quite successful writer, he apparently gets sent stories by young people who want to become writers like him. He stared intently into space at this point and shook his head, his long grey hair wafting this way and that.

'Some of the dross I am sent...' he said as he removed his small circular glasses and started tutting. 'It is,' he continued, 'difficult to believe that you children get any schooling at all in the correct use of English – the finest language in the world, I might add. To say nothing of *thinking* and *writing* creatively.'

There are five of us on the course (Mr Coe only ever takes on five pupils at a time). My fellow creative writers are: Molly Moon (my sometimes best friend – all her creative writing is pony-related), Colin Timpkins (he insists that everyone calls him 'Col' instead of Colin because he thinks it sounds cooler. Everyone still calls him Colin, though. Or 'Timpo' which he also hates), Zoe Brown (very keen and annoyingly good at creative writing) and Jack Drinkwater (I wasn't sure why he was on the course – he never seemed that interested). We are all pupils at St Chad's Middle School and Mr Coe holds his classes in the School library.

After Mr Coe's outburst about the dross he gets sent he fell silent (I think he might have been despairing about the state of English in England). In response, we five grew a little distracted and started looking at each other and then, for want of anything else to do, we all began looking at the books that lined the walls of the library.

'What are you doing?' Mr Coe asked loudly, suddenly back in the room with us. 'I don't hold my classes here in order for you all to stare vacantly into space.'

We fixed our eyes back on Mr Coe and then Molly Moon asked, 'Why do you hold your classes here, Mr Coe?'

He appeared to brighten up a little at this. 'Ah, my Little Inklings,' that's what he calls us, his 'Little Inklings', 'the reason we meet in the library is because we are surrounded by books and,' he paused for dramatic effect, 'osmosis!'

He stood before us with a triumphant look on his face as if he'd told us the secret to eternal life.

We looked blankly at each other.

I raised my hand. 'Mr Coe,' I asked, 'what does osmosis mean?'

'Osmosis is the transference of one thing to another thing via some unseen magical power. Perhaps, by being exposed to the fine books that line the walls here, the wisdom and beauty they contain will be magically transferred to you and so inform and improve your creative writing endeavours.'

'Without actually reading them?' asked Molly.

'Does it work?' I asked.

'That doesn't sound right,' said Colin.

'I don't believe it,' said Zoe.

'What?' mumbled Jack.

We were all talking at the same time so Mr Coe raised his hand to quieten us.

It didn't work – we continued jabbering away.

'Silence!' shouted Mr Coe.

We all piped down.

'Enough! Enough of your incessant logorrhoea.'

I raised my hand again. 'Mr Coe,' I asked, 'what does logorrhoea mean?'

He looked at his watch and said, 'Time's up. If you don't know what logorrhoea means I suggest you avail yourself of a dictionary.'

He often does this. Towards the end of the lesson, he'll come out with a word that none of us Little Inklings knows and then he'll expect us to look it up. I'm quite happy to look up definitions in my dictionary (Molly Moon never does – she asks me at school the next day). I find looking things up easy and enjoyable. The homework that Mr Coe sets for us is the bit that I find difficult. It's always a piece of creative writing and, so far, it has always tested the limits of my imagination. The homework is also usually poetry-related. In fact, poetry is the main topic in all of Mr Coe's lessons. He is very fond of saying, 'You will be aware, I am sure, of Mr Samuel Taylor Coleridge's famous dictum: 'Prose: words in their best order; Poetry: the *best* words in the best order." We're certainly aware of Mr Coleridge's dictum now; Mr Coe repeats it almost every week. So poetry is the focus of the classes and poetry is the subject of our homework.

That week, for example, Mr Coe had set us the challenge of writing a poem about an animal of our choice. After much thought and many, many false starts, I eventually came up with a poem I called *The Happy Tree Frog*:

> *The Happy Tree Frog*
> I am a happy tree frog
> A happy tree frog, me.
> And I spend all my happy days
> Happily up a tree.

Not too bad, I thought as I handed it in to Mr Coe at the start of the following week's lesson, not too bad at all. It rhymes and it gives you a small insight into the living conditions of a tree frog.

It didn't take Mr Coe very long to read it. It took him even less time to mark it.

The Happy Tree Frog was back under my nose within a minute. Below my masterpiece Mr Coe had written five words in bright red ink:

Somewhat juvenile and somewhat short.

Hmmm. I *am* juvenile, I thought. And it's the perfect length.

So the 'creative' bit of the creative writing course is hard - much, much harder than I could ever have imagined. I also appear to be the only one of Mr Coe's five pupils who struggles with the homework. Everyone else seems to be doing fine (including Jack Drinkwater who seems barely conscious most of the time) although the rest of the Little Inklings started in September and I only joined in January so I suppose they had a head start.

Fulfilling my ambition to become the world's greatest storyteller is going to be more difficult than I thought.

By the way, we are not and never will be 'students' in Mr Coe's eyes; we are 'pupils'. He is very fond of saying 'Students study; pupils *learn!*' He's also fond of saying that he will not tolerate any 'Shilly-shallying.' Sadly, whenever I try to work on Mr Coe's homework, I do a fair amount of shillying and an awful lot of shallying.

Before we broke up for the Easter holiday Mr Coe set us the task of writing a poem on the theme of heroism. This could be about a person we thought was heroic or it could be about heroism in general. I have to tell you that it's been pretty much wall-to-wall shilly-shallying from me ever since.

The reason for this is that my hero is a boy in my class called Mark Dangerfield. Mark Dangerfield is brave and kind and wonderful and definitely hero material. Writing about Mark presents no problems at all; I've written loads of poems about him. Poems like this, for example:

> Emmabella Murray, Emmabella Murray
> No need to rush, no need to hurry.
> Your future's bright; your fate is sealed;
> You're going to marry Mark Dangerfield.

Obviously, I'm not going to hand something like that into Mr Coe. Sometimes he makes us read our work out to the others. I know that Mark Dangerfield is my hero but I'm the only one who knows and that's the way I want it to stay.

So who to choose?

I love Mum and Dad but does that make them my heroes? They are heroic for putting up with Finn (so am I!) but I wasn't sure that would count.

By the way, Finn, who spent most of last summer making magic wands that didn't work and a papier-mâché volcano that did, has recently started conducting actual scientific experiments.

In January, Nana Grundy gave him a chemistry set (why, Nana, *why*?) that she'd found in one of the charity shops in town. Ever since then it's been impossible to pass his bedroom door without smelling some new and generally unpleasant smell (it always was, ha, ha). Once, he really did make an actual stink bomb and let it off in the kitchen. We had to open the front and back doors and all the windows to get rid of the smell and it was February and cold. As a result, Mum confiscated the chemistry set but I know for a fact that he's got it back now – I have no idea how.

I know Finn has his chemistry set back because I snuck into his room a couple of weeks ago and saw it sitting on his desk. I thought that he was out so I'd crept into his room to take another look at the mysterious map that hangs on his wall.

Finn's mysterious map is huge and it shows the whole world. It also has a growing number of coloured pins stuck into it at what appear to be random locations. However, I know that there is absolutely nothing random about Finn or the way his mind works which means there'll be nothing random about the positioning of the pins, so I have made it my mission to work out their significance. In part, this is because Finn thinks that he is smarter than me (he is actually) and I want to get one over on him and it's also because I really want to know what the map means.

I had by this time started to make notes about the map in one of my notebooks but that didn't seem to be getting me very far. To date, in my mysterious map investigations, I'd managed to make a note of the following locations:

- Edinburgh, Scotland
- Reykjavik, Iceland
- Florence, Italy
- Skiathos, Greece
- Manila, Philippines
- Abuja, Nigeria
- Edmonton, Canada
- Omaha, USA

My best guess is that it might be some sort of word puzzle that involves rearranging the first letters of the places and/or the countries to find the solution. The problem is that I never seem to get enough time to look at the whole map – as I said, it's huge – and Finn seems to be adding new pins to it all the time.

The more I thought about it the further away from the solution I seemed to get. I just couldn't figure it out.

Sadly, on the day I'd noticed that Finn had got his chemistry set back, I didn't get a chance to continue my investigations. I'd finally reached the map after charting a winding course through all the junk that littered Finn's bedroom floor (traffic cones, old radio parts, his flourishing Venus flytrap on a low handmade table) when I felt a sharp pair of eyes burning into the back of my skull.

I turned around quickly to find Finn standing in the doorway.

'Can I help you?' he asked, evenly.

'No, not really,' I garbled.

'What do you want?'

'I was going to have a look at your map,' I said because it was the only thing I could think of to say.

'Why?'

'Erm... erm... because I've forgotten what the capital of Egypt is.' Hopeless, hopeless, hopeless.

'It's Cairo and that's what the internet is for.'

His hawk-like brown eyes never left me as I carefully threaded my way back across his bedroom floor. I was desperate to get out of there.

'I need to get a lock on my bedroom door,' he said and then he whispered as I squeezed past him in the doorway, 'You'll never work it out.'

He may well be right. He'll certainly be right if he ever gets a lock on his door.

The more I thought about who my hero is the more I came to realise that the one person I should probably choose was Grandpa Grundy. He'd been in the Navy so he'd probably done some fairly heroic things.

> Grandpa Grundy sailed to sea
> In a boat not green or red.
> It was made of metal
> And battleship grey
> Just like the hair on his head.

Or:

> Grandpa Grundy was born on a Monday;

This means he's fair of face.

He spent his life in the Navy,

Protecting the human race.

Better? Hmm. I'm not sure. I don't even know if Grandpa Grundy was born on a Monday which is somewhat important to the composition of the poem (although a Sunday would work, too).

I will stop shilly-shallying and give this more thought.

I'm still going to Art Club after school every Thursday, too. Art Club is interesting and frustrating in equal measure. Some weeks things seem to go very well (my pastel drawing of apples and bananas was something of a triumph, if I do say so myself) and some weeks things go very badly. One week I tried to paint a landscape at sunset (from memory) and it ended up looking more like a slice of streaky bacon.

When Mr Wise, our Art teacher, caught sight of it he said, 'Ah…' and then he said, 'Ah…' again. And then he said, 'Landscapes can be a challenge. Particularly at sunrise…'

'It's a sunset,' I replied, as if that would explain everything.

'Ah…' said Mr Wise, for a third and final time.

I'd spent a lot of last year worrying about Mum and Dad because they hadn't been talking to each other but everything seemed to be fine there, too. They were getting on really well and they seemed happy. More than happy, actually; which was a bit embarrassing at times.

Auntie Maisie continued to fret about things she could have no influence on (the world and the whales), Uncle Dougie continued to bristle as a result of my comprehensive victory over him in our Christmas Monopoly game (in the three times I'd seen him since Christmas he'd refused to speak to me or even acknowledge my presence). Nana and Grandpa Grundy were just the same as usual.

So apart from struggling with Mr Coe's creative writing homework, the first few weeks of the New Year had been peaceful and calm. Everything, for once, seemed exactly as I liked it; everything seemed neatly ordered and arranged...

B is for ...But

...**B**ut it wasn't to last.

One day in January, at morning break, I went out to the playground to see Molly Moon talking and then laughing (*laughing?*) with SOPHIE GALLIMORE. Sophie Gallimore, who Nana Grundy would, quite correctly, describe as a 'bad sort', is *always* trouble.

She shouts a lot in the playground; she accused Alice Conroy of looking at her in a funny way so she pulled her hair *and* she once escaped from school at lunch break because she was bored.

Sophie Gallimore's escape was one of the biggest events in our entire school life. People still talk about it. One minute she was in the playground and the next she was on the other side of the railings, on the pavement and at large in the outside world.

We all thought Sophie would run off but she didn't – at least not at first. She just walked up and down the pavement, smiling, waving and making exaggerated bows to the rest of us (for which read every single child in the school) who had gathered in the playground to watch the spectacle. The teachers soon rushed over once they'd seen what was happening. Sophie winked at them, took one more deep bow and said, 'See you later, suckers,' before turning on her heels and sprinting off down the street like some half-crazed gazelle.

The next day, the playground was buzzing with talk of Sophie Gallimore's Great Escape. Everyone agreed that she was bound to be expelled. She was going to be expelled and she was going to be expelled for good.

But she wasn't. She's still at the school and nobody knows how or why. Her behaviour appears to be no different either.

Whenever I have the misfortune to meet Sophie's laser-like gaze, she looks at me with a smirk – as if she knows more about everything than I do. This may well be true but it's a very unsettling look, all the same.

Since we've been at St Chad's, Sophie has been in the same class as us but we've never had much to do with her. That was until Mr French, our English teacher, set us his metaphor challenge last year. We all got paired up and then we had to describe our partner using metaphors. I was paired with Sophie (*why?*) and she wrote that I look like a duck. In contrast, I was quite kind in my description of her. I could have written that with her raven-black hair, her slightly pointed chin and her small, alert eyes she looks a bit like a rat (a rat with an attitude problem), but I didn't, of course. Whenever our paths have crossed since the metaphor challenge she's called me Duck.

She has a twin brother called Sam who is also a 'bad sort' (he looks a bit 'ratty', too). He doesn't call me 'Duck' whenever he sees me, though; he just smiles and says, 'Hello, Emmabella,' and then looks quickly down at his shoes.

It's all very odd.

Anyway back to the fateful morning in January. Seeing Molly and Sophie huddled together in the chilly morning air made me curious. I knew that Molly would never be friends with Sophie so I walked over to see what was happening.

'Hi,' I said, by way of introduction.

They turned to look at me.

'Hello, Duck,' said Sophie smirkingly.

'Sophie needs some help,' said Molly.

'Does she?' I asked.

'She wants to join Mr Coe's creative writing course.'

'Why?' I asked, surprised (as Mr French's Metaphor Challenge had shown, Sophie didn't appear to be interested in English at all).

'It's something to do,' Sophie replied (with a smirk, of course).

'Well, good luck with that,' I said with a nervous laugh.

'What does that mean?' asked Molly a little sharply (whose side was she on?).

'Well,' I blurted, 'Mr Coe only ever takes five pupils at a time and I had to wait ages for someone to drop out. It's not easy getting on the course.'

'I happen to know,' Molly said to Sophie, 'that Jack Drinkwater's not all that bothered about it. I think it was his mum's idea for him to do it. He'll probably drop out soon. I'll put in a good word for you with Mr Coe.'

I looked at Molly. It was a look that said, 'What?!?'

'Mr C can be a bit strict,' she continued, 'but it's fun. You'll enjoy it.'

I could feel Sophie's eyes burning into me.

'What's wrong with you, Duck?' asked Sophie. 'Are you blushing?'

I did a smart turn and stomped off past the huddled groupings of freezing children in search of somewhere, *anywhere* else where I could be alone to think about what had just happened.

'Hello, Emmabella,' Sam Gallimore said as I hurried past him. He probably followed this by looking at his shoes but I didn't know because I didn't see. I had my head down and my scarf pulled up. My cheeks were red and burning.

C is for Camping

We weren't the only people heading over to the Lake District on Good Friday morning. Uncle Dougie had won a weekend break for four people for being the world's greatest salesman, or something, and he and Auntie Maisie had decided to take Nana and Grandpa Grundy along for a treat. They were staying in a swanky hotel; we were camping down the road.

At the campsite by Derwentwater, Dad drove around looking for a suitable place to pitch the tent. He always did this when we arrived at a new campsite and I never knew why.

'That should do,' he said, pointing to a spot quite close to the lake's gently lapping waters.

I'd like to say that arriving at the campsite is the best part of a camping holiday because the numerous attempts to put the tent up properly haven't started and the arguments haven't begun but as far as I'm concerned, all camping trips are one long nightmare from start to finish so picking one bit as the best part is completely impossible.

I've never understood the attraction of camping. We spend all year in our nice warm house, sleeping in our nice warm beds and then when we get the chance to go away on holiday we end up sleeping on a blow-up mattress under a flappy bit of fabric having to walk miles across a sheep poo-covered field in the middle of the night to get to the toilet. Mum and Dad seem to enjoy it and they're in charge so I have to lump it. I think Finn feels the same way about camping as I do; he has to lump it, too.

I have a theory about life. Life, as I'm sure you know, can be very confusing. Every day I come across things that I don't understand (like the appeal of camping) or don't know (like not knowing how many lakes there are in the Lake District), so to make life less confusing I try to live in a neatly ordered and arranged way. I keep my room tidy, I brush my teeth twice a day and I try to be on time for all my lessons at school. A life lived in a neatly ordered and arranged way should be less confusing and all the better for it.

That's the theory, at least.

The one thing you need to know about camping is that it is definitely *not* neatly ordered and arranged. In fact, it's about as far away from neatly ordered and arranged as it is possible to be. You spend the whole time tripping over things when you're camping. You trip over your clothes, your rucksack, your sleeping bag, your mattress, the camping stove, the cardboard box that Dad brought back from work that sits in the middle of the tent and contains the food rations for the trip. You trip over *everything*. And when you're not tripping over things you're walking into your fellow campmates. It's horrible. And the tent smells dusty, musty and stale, just like our Santa sacks used to smell before they were lost when we moved house last year. It's a pity the tent hadn't been lost in the house move, too. Although if it had have been, Mum and Dad would have bought another one. They *love* camping. What's wrong with them?

Worst of all – the absolute worst thing about camping is that I have to share a sleeping compartment with Finn. You can't call it a room because it's not a room. It's a canvas compartment. Or a canvas cell. Yes, cell is a better word for it.

Finn and I looked on as Dad began unrolling the tent on the damp tufty ground. We didn't offer to help as I don't think either of us wanted to give the impression that we were anything other than *very* unwilling participants in this expedition. Helping to put up the tent would surely have shown a level of acceptance of our situation which neither of us wanted to give. So we both stood in silence, arms folded, and watched.

Just as Dad had the tent unfolded as he liked it, a large house spider came crawling out of one of the folds, scuttling along in the way that spiders do.

Mum is terrified of spiders. Whenever her fear of spiders comes up, people always say to her that there is nothing to worry about – even the big ones that live in the Amazon can give you a bite no worse than a bee sting. Mum gets incredibly annoyed by this; she's not bothered about their size and she's not bothered about the pain they might be able to inflict. She is terrified of the way they move.

So when Mum turned back from the car and saw the spider scuttling over the tent she shrieked, dropped the camping stove she was carrying and yelled, 'Get rid of it!'

A man who we'd never met before was unloading his tent in the spot next to ours. At the sound of Mum's shriek, he came wandering over to see what the problem was.

I'd noticed before that people on campsites assume an immediate level of jolly friendship and chumminess. Perhaps it's because everyone is in the same depressing and disappointing boat – having to spend uncomfortable nights on the ground – that brings it on.

So this man came wandering over to see what was happening. He saw the spider (which Dad was now failing to scoop up in his hands) and he saw Mum's distress and he said, 'It's only a house spider, that can't hurt you-'

I think at this point the man planned to introduce himself to us in the way that campsite people do. He perhaps had in mind shared evening meals around the gas stove and lively conversations about past camping trips.

But that didn't happen. That didn't happen at all.

As soon as he said the words 'that can't hurt you' Mum turned on him and yelled (really, *really* yelled), 'I don't care! It's not about whether or not it can hurt me it's about the way it moves. It's sinister. It's creepy. It's disturbing. Its fangs could be filled with poison and I wouldn't care. Its fangs could be filled with an elixir for eternal life and I still wouldn't care. I don't like the way they move. Got it?'

From the way in which the man, now looking quite pale and shaken, silently backed away from Mum, quickly threw his tent into the boot of his car and drove to a distant part of the campsite I assumed that he had indeed got it.

We never saw him again.

Finn looked at Mum with new-found respect and held up his hand to give her a high five.

'Not now, Finn,' said Mum.

'Sweet,' he replied. 'You're the boss.' And for once, he meant it.

Dad eventually captured the spider and placed it on the other side of the dry stone wall that ran around the edge of the campsite. From the way in which Mum kept nervously glancing over at the wall, this might not have been quite far enough away for her comfort but she didn't say anything. Instead, she tried to help Dad as he began unfolding the tent poles.

And then it started to rain.

Whoever named Good Friday 'Good Friday' had a deeply ironic sense of humour.

Finn and I retreated to the dry of the car. We watched through the rain-lashed windows as Mum and Dad began to argue about the best way to put up the tent. Finn soon tired of this so he pulled *The Art of War* out of his bag, slumped back and started reading. My books were in my bag in the boot of the car (safely out of reach for the journey over to the Lakes). As I continued watching Mum and Dad, my thoughts drifted off to my own recently-developed fear of spiders.

Every night since my photo appeared in the local paper (oh my, just you wait...), I'd had the same disturbing dream and seeing the spider on the tent brought it vividly back to mind. I'm calling it a dream but I could just as easily call it a nightmare.

In the dream, I am running across a huge desert being chased by a massive boulder. I keep running through the endless landscape and all the time the boulder keeps chasing me, getting closer and closer. Running, running, running. Endlessly running onwards, too afraid to look over my shoulder as I hear the boulder getting closer and closer. Until at last, I see through the desert heat haze (it's a very vivid dream) a cliff face rising up from the sand like a mirage. But it's not a mirage, it's real (it's real in the dream, if you know what I mean). As I get closer to the cliff I can see an opening – a cave! Through the heat, I can see that it is surely big enough for me to get into but not big enough for the boulder. I keep on running; faster than I've ever run before. Nearly there, nearly there, and then, at last, the opening is directly in front of me. I dive in, exhausted and out of breath. As I hit the cave floor I hear the boulder smash against the entrance, sealing me in.

As my eyes adjust to the darkness of the cave, I suddenly get an uncomfortable feeling that I'm not alone. Turning over on the cold and dusty cave floor I look up to see a huge hairy spider sitting on its finely spun web a few inches above my head. I shuffle back on my elbows unable to take my eyes off the hideous creature.

'Do not be afraid, human,' the spider says.

Okay, I think, a talking spider. That makes sense.

'At least do not be afraid yet,' continues the spider. 'The time for terror for your kind *will* come. But not yet.'

'That's good to know,' I say.

'Silence, puny human. You have no concept of the horrors we will unleash on you feeble two-legged creatures.'

The spider was right, I didn't. I think better of confirming this, though, since it'd told me to be quiet and called me puny.

'Well?' roars the spider. 'Don't you want to know about our plans for the human race?'

Make your mind up, I think. First, you want me to be quiet and now you're asking me a direct question.

I nod, to be on the safe side.

'We are going to take over the world!' the spider cackles ferociously, its horrible laughter echoing around the bare cave.

I want to say, 'Oh yeah? You and whose army?' but decide that now isn't the time to be flippant. Instead, I say, 'When?'

The spider breathes in deeply, 'I'm not exactly sure,' it says. 'World domination is a big job. It takes a lot of planning.'

'Well,' I say, 'good luck with it.'

'Don't toy with me, human. You'll be as the dust in this desert when we are done with you.'

'Okay.'

'We are patient. We will take our time. We can go for months without eating,' the spider fixed me with all eight of its beady eyes. 'Did you know that?'

I shake my head.

'We will bide our time until the moment is right; then we will rise up and strike and humans will be wiped from the face of the earth forever. House spiders are my surveillance team; tarantulas are my infantry and black widows are my assassins.'

'Who are you?' I ask.

'I,' bellows the spider, 'am King Spider.'

Dust falls from the roof of the cave as King Spider's words rattle around the enclosed space.

'Now go,' says King Spider, 'go and think on your useless future.'

I stay where I am.

'Well? What are you waiting for?'

'I can't go and think on my useless future. There's a great big boulder blocking the entrance to the cave.'

'Ah, yes. Of course.'

King Spider raises one of his eight legs and the boulder magically slides away from the cave's mouth.

I scramble to my feet and run out, out into the light and it is at this moment that I always wake up.

When I first had the dream I woke in a worried sweat but by Good Friday I'd had the same dream for seven nights in a row and was getting quite used to it.

The odd thing was that I had no idea that spiders could go for months without eating but it turns out that this is actually true (I looked it up). Is it possible to know something without knowing that you know it?

Anyway, that's why I've suddenly become scared of spiders. They're plotting to kill us all and take over the world.

D is for Demo

After Christmas, Auntie Maisie found something new to be concerned about (in addition to the trees, the seas and the state of the world in general). The town's Library is threatened with closure because there isn't enough money to go around, apparently, so Auntie Maisie had started a campaign to save it.

One afternoon in March, I was quietly minding my own business at the kitchen table when Mum and Auntie Maisie came bustling in, all of fluster.

'Have you heard, Emmabella?' said Maisie.

I hadn't heard anything and said so.

'They're going to close the Library. For good,' she said.

I had no idea who 'they' were but I could understand the thinking behind closing it. Sadly, it seemed that no one used it. No one apart from me, of course.

I'd been going to the Library more often than usual because I'd discovered a new and wonderful dictionary. It's called *Brewer's Dictionary of Phrase and Fable* and it's great. I saw it one day in the Library and decided to take a look. I'd seen it before but had always passed it over because I'd assumed it was something to do with making beer. However, in January I noticed the words 'phrase' and 'fable' and I had to take a look.

All I can say is, 'What a find!' The Library's version is quite old; it is an exact copy of the second edition of the book which the introduction states was published in 1894 (when Queen Victoria was on the throne).

I carefully carried the heavy book over to one of the Library's empty desks and opened it up. I started at 'A' (obviously) and one of the first entries I came across was 'Abbey-lubber':

> **Abbey-lubber** (*An*). An idle,
> well-fed dependent or loafer.

A couple of entries later I found 'Abbotsford':

> **Abbotsford**. A name given
> by Sir Walter Scott to Clarty
> Hole, on the south bank of
> the Tweed, after it became
> his residence. Sir Walter
> devised the name from a
> fancy he loved to indulge in,
> that the *abbots* of Melrose
> Abbey, in ancient times,
> passed over the *fords* of the
> Tweed.

How very interesting. I had no idea who Sir Walter was and *Brewer's* doesn't say but I could understand why he wanted to change the name of his house from Clarty Hole – that didn't sound very nice.

On the next page I found this:

Abderitan   Laughter.
Scoffing laughter, incessant laughter. So called from Abdéra, the birthplace of Democrîtos, the laughing philosopher.

A laughing philosopher? I thought philosophers were very serious people who spend their time rubbing their chins and thinking weighty things about weighty problems (not that I know very much about philosophers).

This was all very fascinating.

I made a resolution there and then. I was going to read all of *Brewer's Dictionary of Phrase and Fable*. The only slight drawback to this plan is that it's 1,324 pages long so it was going to take me some time. It's also in the 'Reference' section which means I can't borrow it to take it home. My plan meant that I'd have to spend a lot more time in the Library which was no bad thing. I already went about once a week. Now I would have to go more often.

My discovery of *Brewer's* coincided with Sophie Gallimore getting a place on Mr Coe's creative writing course, just as Molly Moon had foretold.

This was in no way a good thing.

The way Sophie had got a place on the course had seemed effortless enough and ever since she'd been there she'd breezed through the various tasks that Mr Coe had set for us. It didn't make any sense.

After Sophie joined the writing class, she and Molly had become firm friends. This, in turn, led to Sophie becoming friends with Penny Tupper, my other sometimes best friend. After school on the day that Auntie Maisie was to bring the bad news about the Library, I saw Molly and Penny ahead of me on the pavement. I was going to run to catch them up when I saw that Sophie was also with them. So I didn't. I held back and mooched behind them as they dallied along the High Street. At the Market Place, I crossed the road and peered up at the Abbey's huge tower. The old stones that made up the Abbey's walls had drawn me back again. I wasn't sure why.

It was March and it was cold and the door to the Abbey was still open so I decided to go in. To be honest, it wasn't much warmer inside but it was peaceful and quiet and it felt like a good place to be. I almost had the place to myself; I could just make out two other people but they were a long way away.

As I got closer I could see that the two figures were Mr and Mrs Coldwell, our other next-door neighbours (on the other side to Mr Oddy) on Cherry Tree Terrace. Even though they are our neighbours I didn't really know them very well. They spend a lot of their time abroad although I don't know why. Anyway, they seem very nice and friendly whenever I do see them so when they noticed me in the Abbey I gave them a little wave and then dodged down the big central aisle.

The interior of the Abbey is massive. It almost seems to be bigger inside than it looks from the outside, if that makes sense. The wide main aisle has walls that shoot straight up to a wooden ceiling. About halfway up the walls is a sort of balcony that runs all the way around. I had no idea how people got up to the balcony or who was allowed up there but I did know that beneath my feet was an ancient and creepy crypt which was more than 1,300 years old. We'd come here on a school trip and they'd taken us down then. Everybody else tried to make their friends jump in the crypt's spooky atmosphere but I didn't – I just stood there taking it all in. I'd never been in such an old place – it was like standing inside history.

I sat down on one of the pews, looked down at my shoes and tried to work out what was going on with Molly, Penny and Sophie. Sophie had never shown any interest in us before and we had never shown any interest in her (apart from when she was doing something outrageously bad like escaping from School). What was happening? Would I have to become friends with Sophie if I wanted to stay friends with Molly and Penny? Did I actually want to stay friends with Molly and Penny? I didn't think I'd want to start making new friends and I'd known Molly and Penny since we'd been at nursery together. On the other hand, I didn't want to be friends with Sophie Gallimore because she was mean and nasty. Maybe Molly and Penny had forgotten this or maybe they didn't care.

I looked up to see a man in a long black robe walking towards me and as he got closer, I could see that he had a big bushy beard. He smiled - at least I think he smiled. It was hard to tell with the big beard covering the lower part of his face. He had very kind eyes, though.

'We have a quiet chapel', he whispered as he reached my pew, 'if you'd like somewhere silent to pray.'

This whole place is silent, I thought. I thanked him, picked up my school bag and headed for the exit.

I hadn't been praying, anyway. Perhaps I should have been.

On my way out I bumped into Mr and Mrs Coldwell.

'It's good to see you in the Abbey,' said Mrs Coldwell.

'I thought I'd pop in,' I replied.

'Good for you,' said Mr Coldwell.

I smiled and said goodbye. Had it been 'good for me'? Too early to tell, I suppose.

Back at home, I slumped down at the kitchen table and that was when Mum and Auntie Maisie scuttled in with the news about the Library.

'Did you hear what I said?'

'Sorry, Auntie Maisie, I drifted off there for a moment. What did you say?'

'I said,' she said, 'I'm arranging a demo against the proposed closure of the Library on Saturday. I'm making banners and T-shirts. You'll lend your support? Please say you will. This is so very, *very* important. We simply can't lose the Library. It would be a travesty. A travesty and a tragedy.'

I wanted to say, 'You're wasting your time, Auntie. No one ever uses it anyway,' but only because I was feeling glum about Sophie Gallimore and my brain was jumbled about what to do about her.

What I actually said was, 'Of course, Auntie, happy to help.'

I *love* the Library. I wouldn't want it to close.

Then Finn wandered in with his hand-decorated school bag (a repeating Paisley pattern of his own design) over his shoulder.

'Ah, Finn,' said Auntie Maisie, 'just the person. As you've no doubt heard, they're planning to close the Library. We simply can't let that happen. I'm organising a demo on Saturday. Can I count on your support?'

Finn shook his head and said, 'You're wasting your time, Auntie. No one ever uses it anyway.'

He helped himself to a biscuit and sloped off to his room.

E is for Easter, of course!

The tent was finally erected by lunchtime on Good Friday. We then set about transferring sleeping bags, inflatable beds, clothes and food from the car into the tent.

In the rain.

The rain looked as if it would continue for the rest of the day. As Dad inflated the beds, Mum looked out of the unzipped tent door and brightly asked, 'What shall we do after lunch?'

'Let's walk into Keswick,' said Dad.

So after a quick lunch of sausages and beans cooked over the gas camping stove the four of us tramped into Keswick.

We looked around the town and dodged into some of the shops when the rain changed from light drizzle to complete downpour; which was often. In one of the many outdoor equipment shops, I bought a bar of Kendal Mint Cake. Dad said it was the sweetest substance known to man but it was just the thing you needed if you were going to climb a mountain.

And that was exactly what I was going to do.

Easter Saturday had been pencilled in as the day when we were going to climb a mountain called Outerside. I couldn't wait.

Ever since the Day of My Great Humiliation (about which more, much more, soon – even though, whenever I think about it, it makes my *brain* blush) my neatly ordered and arranged life had been disastrously knocked off course. Before we came over to the Lake District I'd decided that some fresh air might help lift the doomy gloom I'd found myself in and the best place to get the freshest air of all, I'd thought, would be on top of a mountain.

As well as being full of lakes, the Lake District is also full of mountains so I was sure climbing one of them wouldn't be too difficult. Mum and Dad both seemed keen (Finn less so); in fact, Dad lent me an old set of books that he'd had for a long time all about the mountains in the Lake District.

The seven little books that make up *A Pictorial Guide to the Lakeland Fells* were written and illustrated with lots of little drawings by a man called A. Wainwright. I started with 'Book Six' which is all about the North Western Fells since these were the hills that seemed closest to where we would be staying.

Flicking through the small book I discovered that there was a mountain called Outerside. I liked the name immediately because it sounds a bit like 'outside' (which was exactly where I wanted to be) but more so. Not just 'outside' but Out*er*side. This, and the fact that I'd been feeling like an outsider at school (an outcast, in fact), made me think that Outerside might be the mountain for me.

I almost had second thoughts about this, though, when I began to read Mr Wainwright's description: 'Outerside springs quite steeply from the abyss…' Abyss? That sounded scary. '…of Coledale, and in less distinctive company it would attract much attention. As it is, visitors rarely tread its pleasant summit.' It almost sounded perfect apart from the 'abyss' bit.

Mr Wainwright's little drawing of the hill was nice, though. He'd sketched it in the winter with snow on the ground – on a path next to the hill were a pair of footprints in the snow. Next to the footprints, he'd written: 'The Abominable Snowman? No, only the author (not that there's much difference).' I was growing to like Mr Wainwright.

My concerns about the abyss were soon calmed when I turned the page. Here, A. Wainwright describes and illustrates the route to the summit from a village called Stair (a strange name for a village but it was close to where we would be staying): 'Outerside is very steep frontally, facing Coledale, and, when viewed from that valley, the possibility of reaching its top by easy walking is inconceivable. This route from Stair, however, provides that simple access.'

That sounded more like it. The hill couldn't be climbed frontally so I'd have to climb it backally.

I had found my mountain and I had found my route. Solutions to all my problems would, I was sure, be found at the top of Outerside.

Back to Keswick on Good Friday. As we reached the end of the main street I felt as if I'd visited every outdoor adventure shop in the world and it was at that point that I saw a little sign pointing down a side street. The little sign read 'Pencil Museum'.

A museum about pencils? Could it *actually* be true?

I pointed the sign out to Mum and Dad who looked at each other and nodded. Mum and Dad may have been more interested in its potential as a shelter from the rain but I wasn't bothered about that. Not only was it a museum, it was also a museum about *pencils*. Pencils are my third favourite items of stationery ever (after the fountain pen I was given at Christmas and normal everyday pens).

Good Friday was getting closer to its name.

The Pencil Museum is actually a thing! And what a thing it is. Outside there is an old pencil delivery van and inside there is everything you could ever want to know about pencils.

After we'd bought our tickets the lady behind the counter gave me and Finn a quiz sheet to fill in and told us that if we got all the answers right we'd get a prize at the end. All the answers can be found in the museum which is reached via a low, dark tunnel

(Dad bumped his head twice as we were going through – immediately after the two 'Mind Your Head' signs).

Once you're through the tunnel you can learn all about the mine where they used to get the graphite, the history of the factory where they make the pencils and there is also an information board explaining 'The Fourteen Steps to Pencil Perfection'. From this, I learned that the metal thing that holds a rubber to the end of a pencil is called a (word of the day alert) 'ferrule'.

There are glass display cases containing lots of old pencil sets and a model of a Spitfire hanging from the ceiling. I'm still not sure why this is there. Best of all is The World's Largest Pencil which takes up the whole of the centre of the display area. It's huge!

Believe me, if you like pencils then this is definitely the place for you.

I read the information panels carefully and managed to answer all sixteen questions on the quiz sheet correctly (aren't I good!). My prize was a set of six sketching pencils and a packet of erasers. Brilliant!

Finn didn't enjoy the visit at all and this was reflected in the answers he wrote on his quiz sheet. Here's a flavour:

> Pencils are traditionally made
> from California cedar wood,

how many pencils can one
tree make?
*Trees can't make pencils. You
need a factory and a semi-skilled
workforce for that.*

What was the punishment
for stealing graphite?
Beheading.

Before rubbers, what was
used to erase pencil marks?
Tippex.

In pencils, what does 'HB'
stand for?
Hyper Boring.

The quiz sheet was titled (pencil joke alert) 'What's
the Point' and beneath this Finn had written, 'I keep
asking myself the same question.'

When he handed his sheet in at the end the lady
behind the counter looked it over, handed it back
and said, 'You've not quite got them all right, I'm
afraid. You'll have to try again next time you come.'

'Yeah, like *that's* going to happen,' Finn replied
under his breath.

It was still raining so Mum encouraged me and
Finn to look around the museum gift shop. She also
gave us both a little bit of money to buy a souvenir.

After much thought and consideration, I bought a
brilliant pencil sharpener. It is square-shaped with a
handle on the side and it clips on to a desk. You

push a blunt pencil into the front and then turn the handle and as if by magic the pencil is perfectly sharpened. Mr French has a similar one on his desk at School. Perhaps he'd been to the Pencil Museum, too.

Finn had a very brief glance around the shop and quickly decided not to buy anything. 'There is nothing deserving of my coin here,' he declared loudly.

'That was great, thanks,' I said to Mum and Dad when we were back outside.

Finn pulled up his hood, pushed his hands into his coat pockets and said, 'Where are we going next? The International Museum of Spiral-Bound Notebooks?'

Back at the campsite, Mum and Dad made a sausage casserole (more sausages) under the tent awning. Once we'd eaten and washed up, there didn't seem to be anything else to do so we all went to bed.

Finn and I were in our zipped-up compartment and Mum and Dad were in theirs. As I lay in my sleeping bag on my inflatable mattress I tried to get to sleep but it was impossible with the rain beating down on the outside of the tent. I thought of Auntie Maisie and Uncle Dougie and Nana and Grandpa Grundy in their nice dry hotel and wondered what they were doing.

Sleep was made even more difficult when Finn started rapping in time to the falling rain.

He started off with drum-type sounds – 'Dush! Dush! Dush!' – to the rhythm of the pounding rain. Mum told him to be quiet but that didn't work.

'Dush! Dush! Dush! Boom! Boom! Boom!'

And then he came up with a proper rap:

> 'Rain hits the tent,
> Hit! Hit! Hit!
> I've reached the conclusion
> This holiday is sh-'

'Fionton!' yelled Mum.

Mum only ever called Finn by his full name when she was very mad at him but at least she'd stopped him from completing his rap. However, from the grumblings that I heard from our tented neighbours, it appeared that she'd also woken up the rest of the campsite.

I sat up with a start in the night having dreamed about King Spider so when I woke for a second time on Easter Saturday I didn't feel like I'd had much sleep. Not that it mattered; today was the day we were going to climb Outerside. Finally, I thought, some mountain air to clear my befuddled head.

I could smell bacon frying on the camping stove so I threw on my walking jacket and went out to join the others. Dad was at the frying pan, sheltering under the awning. As he cooked he looked out at the bleak, grey-curtained mountains. The rain hadn't stopped and clouds had descended in the night and now capped the tops of the hills. Each hill seemed to have sprung a new waterfall in the night; they fell like white ribbons down the hillsides into the valleys below.

Dad looked at me and smiled. 'Sorry, Emmabella. I think we'd better postpone the Outerside climb. It wouldn't be safe with the clouds this low.'

He saw the disappointed look on my face.

'Don't be sad, there's always tomorrow.'

'What if the weather's still bad?'

'I'm sure it'll be fine tomorrow.' He looked up at the sky. 'It'll have to stop raining sometime.'

He didn't look convinced.

Finn had not been interested in climbing Outerside so Auntie Maisie had agreed to look after him. She picked him up after breakfast and they headed off in the direction of Keswick. Nana and Grandpa Grundy were also pottering about in Keswick; I had no idea what Uncle Dougie was doing.

Instead of our Outerside climb, Mum, Dad and I drove to Buttermere which is not a *lake* lake, but a *mere* lake (although it's actually very lovely so it could be described as being more than a *mere* lake. Or more than a *mere* mere). As we walked around Buttermere's shoreline we had our hoods up as the rain continued to fall. I spent most of the day looking up at the low clouds covering the tops of the hills that circled the lake. How I wanted to be up there. But it wasn't to be, at least not on Easter Saturday. Dad was right; it wouldn't have been safe.

As we walked around the far end of Buttermere the wind really got up. Out of nowhere, a fiercely strong gust bashed against me knocking me off my feet and into a fence. As Dad helped me up I looked to the sky and saw that the clouds were skittering about above the small valley. Now and then the tops of the hills could be glimpsed through a small break in the racing clouds; the peaks didn't look that far away but they were, today, at least, completely out of reach.

As we turned back towards the small village where we'd parked the car, the rain continued to do its best to dampen my spirits, but I wasn't going to let it. The air was fresh, the waterfalls running down the hillsides were growing more dramatic by the minute and it wasn't school where, in the run-up to Easter, I'd felt like I was suffocating. It was wonderful.

Good weather can make a bad day better, but bad weather can't ruin a good day. And that's what that Easter Saturday in the Lake District was; it was a good day.

After the walk, we went into Keswick to meet Nana and Grandpa and Finn for fish and chips. As part of Uncle Dougie's prize for being super good at whatever it is that he does he'd won a romantic meal for two at a posh restaurant so he and Auntie Maisie were probably drinking champagne and eating caviar as we queued outside the chip shop.

Finn hadn't said a word since we'd met up so I asked him what was wrong.

'Nothing,' he said sullenly.

'Good day?' I asked.

'No,' he replied.

'We had a good day,' I said. 'We walked all the way around Buttermere and I got blown off my feet by a surprise gust of wind.'

'Whoopee doo,' said Finn.

'Sometimes the clouds parted and I could see the tops of the mountains.'

'Sounds thrilling,' he replied.

'What did you do?'

He stayed silent.

'Auntie Maisie must have taken you somewhere.'

'She did,' he replied grimly.

'Where?'

His face was a scowl as he looked up and said, 'She took me to the Pencil Museum.'

He wandered off to stare blankly through the window of a fudge shop.

Oh dear. Poor Finn.

F is for Floating

Easter Sunday is usually quite a nice day. Finn and I have too much chocolate in the morning while Dad cooks roast lamb and his roast potatoes for lunch. In the afternoon we sit at the kitchen table and play a board game. This year we were not having a nice roast lamb lunch because we were camping. This year we were going to have fish paste sandwiches for lunch and Campfire Chilli later.

This was my first thought when I woke up for the second time on Easter Sunday morning (I had, of course, already woken up once in the middle of the night at the end of the King Spider dream). My second thought was: something's not right here.

The rain wasn't drumming on the tent roof which meant that it had at last stopped. This was good news – we'd be able to climb Outerside. But that wasn't it. There was something else. I couldn't put my finger on what it was but something was definitely making me feel uneasy.

And then it hit me.

I was floating.

I looked over to Finn who was still asleep in his sleeping bag on his inflatable mattress. He was bobbing gently up and down.

Perhaps I'm still asleep, I thought; perhaps this is a dream. This might have been true if Dad was also in my dream, sloshing about in water and saying 'Damn! Damn! Damn!'

The zip on the flappy door of our compartment opened and Dad poked his head through.

'You'd better get up, Emmabella. We're flooded.'

I looked over to Finn who had woken up at the sound of Dad's voice. He lay back in his sleeping bag and stared at the roof of the tent as he continued to bob up and down. 'Trippy,' he said.

Dad went back outside and I could hear him muttering to Mum about how the flood was 'pretty biblical.' This was quite appropriate as it was Easter Sunday.

The rain that had been falling steadily since we'd arrived on Good Friday morning had swelled the streams that tumbled down from the hilltops. The streams made the water in the lakes rise. We were camped on the banks of one of the lakes. As we had slept, Derwentwater had risen and risen and that was why we found ourselves floating on our inflatable mattresses on Easter Sunday morning.

Finn and I moved to higher ground while Mum and Dad, knee-deep in water, dismantled the tent. I was still desperate to climb Outerside but I was also hoping that the flood might signal the end of the camping trip. No such luck, unfortunately. Dad was already scoping out a suitable new place to pitch the tent.

And then Nana and Grandpa Grundy arrived bearing more bad news. Auntie Maisie had food poisoning (perhaps it was the caviar).

'Is she all right?' asked Mum.

'Difficult to tell,' said Grandpa, 'she's taken up residence in the bathroom.'

'It'll soon pass through,' said Nana.

'I'd better go and see if she's okay,' said Mum.

Dad threw her the car keys and she was off. Nana and Grandpa Grundy headed to the church in Keswick and Finn tagged along with them which left me and Dad and a very soggy tent in a very soggy field.

The holiday was as far away from neatly ordered and arranged as it was possible to be and my hopes of climbing a mountain were diminishing by the second.

As Dad continued to dismantle the tent he looked over to me and saw the disappointment on my face.

'You really want to climb a hill, don't you?' he asked.

I nodded. 'It doesn't matter though. There'll be another time.'

'Hang on,' he said. 'I've got an idea.'

He took out his phone and made a call.

'Hi Dougie, it's Harvey… Yes, yes, we're fine. Well, we're flooded out actually but I'm dealing with that now. How's Maisie..? Oh dear, she's still in the bathroom? I'm sure she'll be out soon… Oh. You're in there with her. Tell her we're thinking of her… Angelica's on her way over to you and I'm sure she'll be happy to look after Maisie… No, no I don't need any help with the tent. There is something you can do for me, though – well, for Emmabella. She wants to climb a hill and I can't let her go on her own.'

There was a very long pause and then Dad said:

'Yes, you.'

There was an even longer pause and then Dad said:

'As I said, Angelica's on her way over to you. Nana and Grandpa have taken Finn to church and I've got to sort out this sodden tent.'

The pause seemed to last forever and then Dad said:

'You're the only one who can help. I'm sure it won't take long.'

I thought the battery on Dad's phone might run out but eventually he got a response.

'That's great, Dougie, thanks. You've made her day. See you soon.'

Dad put his phone back in his pocket and turned to me, 'Dougie will climb the hill with you.'

'Great,' I replied.

I tried to mean it.

G is for Good Thing

Two weeks before the Easter weekend I joined Auntie Maisie and her fellow campaigning friends on the demo to protest against the closure of the Library. She called round to collect me on Saturday morning and told me how much she really, *really* appreciated my help and that what we were doing was a very 'Good Thing'.

On our way to the park, we called next door to collect Mr Oddy. 'As Finn couldn't help I was one short,' said Auntie Maisie, 'Mr Oddy kindly agreed to step in.'

Mr Oddy's first name is Nigel and that's why Dad calls him Noddy but not to his face. Finn calls him Noddy all the time (including to his face) but that's because he and Mr Oddy bonded over a mega blaster gun battle on Christmas Day. Mr Oddy and I have never bonded over any gun battles so that's why I call him Mr Oddy.

Auntie Maisie had been busy making placards with the words 'Save Our Library' on them. She also had fourteen white T-shirts – one for each of the protestors. Each T-shirt was printed with a single big black letter which, when we were all lined up in the right order, would also spell out 'Save Our Library'.

As we walked through the park to the bandstand where we were due to meet our fellow protestors, Maisie handed one T-shirt to Mr Oddy and one to me.

Mr Oddy pulled his over his head, looked down at it and said, 'Oh. I'm an 'O'!'

'So you are,' I replied, 'very fitting.'

'Actually,' said Mr Oddy, 'I don't think it fits me very well at all.'

'No,' I said, 'that's not what I meant. You're an 'O'; O for Oddy.'

'Oh, yes, of course. Well spotted, Emmabella.'

At the bandstand, everyone else pulled their T-shirts over their heads and we set off, up and out of the park to the Library across the road. As we went along, we joined in with a protest chant that Auntie Maisie had come up with:

Auntie Maisie: 'What do we want?'

The rest of us: 'To borrow books!'

Auntie Maisie: 'When do we want it?'

The rest of us: 'All the time!'

We continued to chant as we walked down the street to the Abbey. Auntie Maisie knew the Market Place would be busy on a Saturday morning so the plan was to line up outside the Abbey and wave our placards there.

During a break in the chanting, Auntie Maisie thanked me again for helping out and told me that a reporter and a photographer from *The Bugler*, our local newspaper, were going to come along to cover our campaign. 'That is the *most* important thing,' said Maisie. 'It is so, *so* important to get media coverage for this sort of thing.'

I was just excited that my picture might be in the paper; I'd never been in *The Bugler* before. Molly Moon's photo was in the paper all the time – usually for something pony-related. Hardly a week goes by without me seeing Molly grinning out from a photo on one of *The Bugler's* pages. I don't know why they bother because the photos are always the same. Molly – wide smile, white teeth, blue eyes, perfectly blonde pony-tailed hair cascading out of the back of her riding helmet – holds the reins of her pony (Blossom) in one hand and in the other she'll be holding up the rosette she's got for winning whatever it is that she's won. Molly is an absolute rosette-magnet; one of the walls of her bedroom is covered in them.

Penny Tupper had been in the paper, too. Last summer, her dog, Harry, won the Waggiest Tail competition at the County Fair and the following week there she was beaming out of one of *The Bugler's* pages with her arms tightly wrapped around poor Harry's neck. Even Sophie Gallimore had had her photo in the paper after she'd won the junior section of the town's fun run a couple of years ago. Spring-heeled Sophie might be a bad sort but she can certainly run fast.

So, of my closest friends (and Sophie) I was the only one who had never been in the paper.

At the Abbey, we lined up across from the market stalls in our letter-printed T-shirts. We shuffled around until we'd got ourselves in the right order and we spelt out, 'Save Our Library'. It took a little while but we got there in the end.

After a bit more chanting and placard waving the reporter from *The Bugler* turned up to interview Auntie Maisie. After a few questions, I overheard Maisie asking the reporter if the photographer was coming too.

'He's already been,' the reporter replied.

Fantastic! I thought. I'm going to be in the paper – fame at last.

After a while, we stopped chanting our protest song – no one seemed to be paying any attention to us. There were plenty of people in the Market Place but they all seemed to be shopping and chatting and generally ignoring our very important demonstration. Their lack of interest must have infected us because we ended up looking at each other and realising that we were only chanting our protest song to each other. So the singing fizzled out like a snuffed candle.

'Well done, everyone,' said Auntie Maisie as she thanked us for about the fiftieth time. 'Now remember,' she continued, 'the press has been here so we'll be in the paper and that is the most important thing. As we all know, media coverage is *absolutely* crucial to our campaign. An article in *The Bugler* will give us the profile we need. Thank you again.'

Auntie Maisie's little speech signalled the end of the demo so I walked home with Mr Oddy.

'I've never been in the paper before,' he said as we walked back through the park.

'Neither have I,' I replied.

'I can't say I've ever wanted to be in the paper,' he said, a little sadly.

In terms of conversation that was it really.

Luckily it didn't take us long to get home and once I was back in my room I sat at my desk, opened my notebook and wrote a poem about Mr Oddy.

> *Ode to Mr Oddy*
> I wandered home with Mr Oddy
> A T-shirt covered his upper body.
> He never wanted to be a 'somebody';
> He was happily content to be a 'nobody'.

But I wasn't content to be a 'nobody'. I wanted to be famous and in my small home town the way you became famous was by having your picture in *The Bugler*.

Sometimes, when you're waiting for something that you *really* want, time seems to pass so very slowly. That's how it was for me when I was waiting for the paper to come out. The protest was on the Saturday and *The Bugler* wasn't published until the Thursday – five whole days to wait. I was patient – I didn't have any choice – and I was also excited. Soon everyone would see my face in the paper.

On the Thursday after the protest, I set off for school five minutes earlier than usual so that I could call at the newsagents to get a copy of *The Bugler*. I'd also factored in the time I thought I would need to sit on a bench in the park and flick through the paper to find my picture.

As it turned out, I didn't have to flick through the paper at all. Our photo was on the front page. The headline read 'Library Protestors Need to Borrow a Dictionary' and beneath that, spread across the entire top half of the front page was the photo of Auntie Maisie, me and the rest of the protestors.

I don't know whether the photographer did it on purpose or whether he had to rush off to some other important photographic assignment but the picture that appeared on the front of *The Bugler* was not of us all lined up spelling the words 'Save Our Library'. Oh no. The photographer had captured us as we arrived outside the Abbey and were shuffling about to get in the right order. So instead of spelling out what we should have been spelling out, we were spelling out something completely different.

The photograph on the front page of *The Bugler* had me, Auntie Maisie and the other protestors in a jumbled line clearly spelling out:

'YOUR A SILVER BRA'.

I was the 'R' in 'BRA' in case you're wondering.

This is an anagram. An anagram is when you use the letters from a word or words to make a different word or different words.

So the photograph had us all spelling 'YOUR A SILVER BRA'. It was also going to spell complete and utter disaster for me.

As I forlornly folded the newspaper I noticed that Mr Oddy's face was obscured by one of the placards so he'd got away with it. Lucky, lucky Mr Oddy.

I pushed the newspaper into the back of my school bag and prayed that no one else at school would ever see the photo, although I knew there was absolutely no chance of that happening. Everyone in the town got *The Bugler*. It was going to be a nightmare.

The rest of the school day was quiet because, of course, no one else had bought a paper on their way to school (why would they?). I was the only one who'd done that, so I was the only one who knew of the shame and embarrassment that was going to rain down on my head.

'I see you got your picture in the paper,' said Dad as soon as I got home after school.

'I don't want to talk about it.'

'That makes sense,' he replied as I ran up the stairs to my room.

I was tidying my room (it didn't really need tidying) in an effort to push my impending humiliation to the back of my mind when Finn swanned in.

'What does 'your a silver bra' mean?' he asked.

'Shut up,' I replied.

'Is it some sort of code?'

'It means that the stupid photographer took the stupid photo at the wrong stupid time and the stupid newspaper stupidly decided to print it.'

'No,' said Finn, 'it means you're going to get the mickey taken out of you big time.'

'Do you think I don't know that?'

He tapped his nose with his finger, said, 'Forewarned is fore-armed,' and left me to my misery.

He was right, of course. I knew that by the next day many of my fellow pupils would have seen the photo and those that hadn't would have heard about it. Gossip runs through St Chad's Middle School like the blue veins run through that horrible cheese that Dad's so keen on.

So, at my desk, in my room, beneath the salmon pink ceiling, I came up with my very own embarrassment-avoidance plan.

To be honest, it wasn't a very good plan and it only involved putting off the inevitable. But it was the best I could come up with.

So the next day I arrived at school almost, but not quite, late. I hung around outside the school gate until I heard the bell ring and the playground clear. Only then did I enter the yard and make for the door. I thought I'd succeeded in not having to face anyone before class but I hadn't. Sophie Gallimore (who else?) *was* late and as she sprinted past me in the playground she called out, 'Silver Bra', and then laughed long and hard.

Sophie's laughter had a definite Abderitan flavour to it.

Our first lesson was English with Mr French. Everyone else was sitting in their places when I tried to quietly (invisibly, actually) enter the room. The muffled sniggers that greeted my arrival proved that my prediction had come true. Everyone had either seen the photograph or heard about it.

At the end of the lesson, Mr French asked me to stay behind.

'I saw your picture in the paper,' he said.

'Of course you did,' I replied, glumly.

'No, no,' he said, 'I thought it was very commendable, giving up your time to try to save the Library. Well done you.'

'Thanks,' I said, my mood brightening a little.

'But I do think you should tell your fellow campaigners that in the context in which it was used, 'your' is spelt wrongly.'

'I know.'

'You see, what you're doing in that instance is conflating two words, 'You' and 'Are'.

'I know.'

He wrote the words 'You' and 'Are' on the whiteboard as he continued, 'So, you remove the 'A' from 'Are', replace it with an apostrophe and join the two words together. And there it is, 'You're'.'

'I KNOW!' I almost stamped my foot as I said this.

'I know that you know,' said Mr French, a small smile breaking across his face.

'I'm going to get teased, aren't I?'

'Mercilessly,' he replied. 'But it'll pass. Look on it as character building.'

But I didn't want my character building. I just wanted a quiet, neatly ordered and arranged life.

I crept out of the school's main door into the playground where my fellow pupils were playing and shouting and generally doing all the things they normally did at break times. I kept my head down low to try to give the impression that the terrified person walking out of the school wasn't really me.

But of course, everyone knew it was me.

Looking back on it, I'm sure the *whole* school didn't fall silent when I walked through the door, but that's how it felt at the time.

I still had my head down so I had no idea who was the first person to shout out 'Silver Bra!' but it didn't matter. The first to say it was the first of many and, like a horrid echo, the words 'Silver Bra' immediately swept around the yard.

Looking up, I saw my so-called friends with Sophie Gallimore gossiping and pointing at me from their usual spot by the railings. I looked away and walked off in the opposite direction.

I walked on by the various groups and gangs that were spread across the entire playground. I passed the sporty kids in the dead centre of the playground and the quiet readers in the shadow of the school's high walls. Out on their own in a far corner, well away from civilised society, were the saddos and the weirdos. Perhaps I should go and join them.

But I didn't. I walked on, skirting the technos, the gossips and the non-sporty kids (the Geeks, the Leaks and the Weaks as Finn calls them).

Finn was there, too. I spotted him in his usual place by the school gate (as close to the exit as it was possible to be) with his disciples gathered around him. He caught my eye as I hurried by and I'm sure that for the briefest moment a look of sympathy and understanding washed across his face. But he didn't call out to me and he didn't come over to see how I was. I understood that. Any display of support for me then would have broken all the rules that govern our brother/sister co-existence.

Those two nasty words - Silver Bra - continued to swirl around the playground so I kept going onward; onward on what felt like the longest walk of my life. Eventually, I found a quiet and secluded spot behind the Science and Technology block.

At lunchtime, I sat with Molly, Penny and Sophie because there was nowhere else to sit. They talked to me in a fairly normal way but every now and then one of them would slip the words 'Silver Bra' into the conversation and they'd all collapse in giggles.

I didn't finish my lunch. Back out in the playground, the words I was dreading continued to be whispered (and occasionally shouted) in my direction. I went back to the Science and Technology block.

There was a new development in my public humiliation at afternoon break. Somebody came up with a song to celebrate my shame (it is sung to the tune of The Camptown Races):

> Emmabella Silver Bra
> Doo da, Doo da
> Emmabella Silver Bra
> Oh, doo da day!

At home, that night, after the first day of my disgrace I didn't eat much at dinner and went up to my room after we'd all finished eating. I tried to read but it was impossible to concentrate.

I caught sight of myself in the mirror. I looked different, I thought. My mousy hair was still the same colour and my slightly pointed nose still had a few faint traces of last summer's freckles (as it always did). My mouth, a little droopy at the sides, was perhaps more droopy. I stared into my brown eyes. They were dry which was important. I hadn't cried and I was determined not to cry.

Above my eyes and below my fringe was a frown, deep and ridged and certainly a result of what had happened at school. That was why I looked different; I looked worried. I would have to be brave and I would have to be strong.

I hated being teased, though. Whenever Sophie Gallimore called me Duck that didn't feel like teasing. That was the name she called me; not that she was calling me that anymore. She, like *everyone* else, was calling me Silver Bra (or just Bra when three syllables proved too challenging for her) and that *did* feel like teasing and it felt a lot worse than being called Duck. It made me the centre of attention (in a bad way) and it served to remind me of what a complete fool I had been for wanting to see my photo in the paper.

The only thing I wanted now was for it all to go away.

Later, in bed, unable to read and unable to sleep I lay back and stared up at my ceiling. Like two cymbals crashing together, the words 'Silver Bra! Silver Bra! Silver Bra!' clanged around my head.

I must have fallen asleep at some point. I woke up with a start in the dark, silent hours of the middle of the night. I was sweating and scared.

That was the night I first dreamed about King Spider and his plan to wipe out the human race.

There were four days of school the next week before we broke up on the Thursday before Good Friday. My 'Silver Bra' situation didn't improve at all.

I continued to be the centre of attention which was horrible. It didn't feel like I was living my own life at all (and it was in no way neatly ordered and arranged), it felt like I was starring in a film of my life. Everything I did at school was being watched and judged and laughed at.

I was a figure of fun. Sniggers greeted my entrance into all my classes and 'Silver Bra' shouts met my appearance in the playground. I continued to seek out the sanctuary of the Science and Technology block.

I returned there to that solitary spot at every break time until we broke up for the holiday.

H is for Hunter Dunn (Joan)

Uncle Dougie was grumpy when, having parked his car at the side of a lane outside the village of Stair, he discovered that he had no signal on his mobile phone. I had no idea who might desperately need to call him on Easter Sunday morning but it certainly made him miserable. Perhaps he was thinking about Auntie Maisie and her upset tummy too, but Mum would be looking after her now, so I was sure he didn't have to worry.

I tried to make conversation to cheer him up.

'This should be fun,' I said.

He huffed and puffed and grunted.

I tried again. 'At least it's stopped raining.'

'This is the Lake District,' he said, darkly. 'If it's not raining it means it's about to rain.'

Perhaps no conversation was a better course to follow.

I have discovered a new poet. Well, he's not really new, he's old (dead, in fact – but don't let that put you off). He's called Sir John Betjeman and, as with all the best poets, most of his poems rhyme (always a good sign).

Mr Coe has been encouraging us to read lots of poetry and he suggested that I might enjoy John Betjeman and he was right. At first, I thought it must be spelt 'Betchman' because that's how it sounds but Mr Coe wrote the name down so I wouldn't have any trouble finding his books in the Library. And I didn't have any trouble; I found *The Best of Betjeman* in the Library's small poetry section.

I was reminded of one of Mr Betjeman's poems as we began the climb up Outerside. It's called *On a Portrait of a Deaf Man* and this is the first verse:

> The kind old face, the egg-shaped head
> The tie, discreetly loud,
> The loosely fitting shooting clothes,
> A closely fitting shroud.

I like the way that Sir John is writing about a deaf man but describes his tie as being 'discreetly loud'. I don't know whether it was possible to be discreet (which means quiet, I think) and loud at the same time. It's not a word I'd expect to find in a description of someone who can't hear. Clever chap, Betjeman.

Anyway, as Dougie and I climbed onwards and upwards I was reminded of the poem's third verse:

> He took me on long silent walks
> In country lanes when young,
> He knew the name of ev'ry bird
> But not the song it sung.

The poor old deaf man.

In a way, I knew how John Betjeman felt. I was on a long silent walk, too, but not because I was walking with a deaf man. My walk was silent because I was with Uncle Dougie and he didn't seem interested in talking at all.

But that didn't stop me from trying again to make some conversation; walking along in silence was getting a bit embarrassing, after all. It wasn't as embarrassing as being the 'R' in 'BRA' in a photo in *The Bugler* but it was uncomfortable all the same.

'So,' I said, 'Auntie Maisie isn't feeling very well?'

'Food poisoning,' he replied.

'What did she eat?'

'Mushroom stroganoff.'

'Did you have that?'

He scoffed at this. 'Hardly.'

A good fifteen minutes and many steps had passed when Dougie said, 'I had the rib-eye steak. Rare.' He stomped off ahead of me.

We continued climbing up the old mine road that leads to Outerside. On our left was a deep valley through which a stream fell in a series of small waterfalls. The higher we climbed the stronger the wind blew, but that didn't matter. And it didn't matter that Uncle Dougie was being a long-faced old grumpy-guts, either. The important thing was that I was climbing a mountain.

As we continued on I thought about my other favourite John Betjeman poem. This one is called *A Subaltern's Love Song*. It's about a man (the subaltern, I suppose. Note to self, look up what a subaltern is) who plays tennis against a woman called Miss Joan Hunter Dunn and then they go back to her house and drink gin and lime before driving to a dance at a golf club and then they don't go to the dance in the end, they just sit in the car and talk and then the subaltern proposes to Miss Joan Hunter Dunn and they end up engaged.

Much as I'd wanted to climb a hill I hadn't expected to be climbing a hill with Uncle Dougie and it wasn't much fun. Part of me began to wish that I was somewhere else. As we carried on climbing I imagined that I was Miss Joan Hunter Dunn ('Furnish'd and burnish'd by Aldershot sun'), and my days were filled with tennis matches against subalterns and gin and lime (well, perhaps lemonade and lime) and golf club dances and long conversations in old cars.

As I reached a ridge, I could, at long last, see Outerside's summit up ahead. But when we reached that summit I realised that it wasn't the real summit (Grandpa Grundy told me later that this is what is known as a 'false summit'). The real summit was far, far higher up and further away.

We trudged on in silence.

I is for Infamous

The Saturday after *The Bugler* with the disastrous picture was published I decided to make one of my occasional visits to see Grandpa Grundy. I was feeling wounded and ashamed and was trying to avoid people like Finn (he thought all his Christmases had come at once), my so-called friends and anyone else who knew me. In short, apart from Grandpa Grundy, I was trying to avoid every other human being on the planet.

So I came up with a plan. As I'd have to cross the park, the Market Place and walk down the High Street (always busy on a Saturday afternoon) a disguise was needed. Even though it was March and the weather was getting less chilly I decided to wrap up warm. I put on my winter coat, wound a woollen scarf around my neck and chin, pulled on a bobble hat and put my hood up for good measure. As only my eyes were visible through the scarf, hat and hood combination nobody could possibly see that it was me.

It was a good plan in theory. It turned out to be somewhat less than good in practice.

I hadn't realised quite how much spring was springing in the world outside. In the park, daffodils were blooming and in the fields that surrounded the town baby rabbits and little lambs were no doubt frolicking in the warm sunshine. It wasn't just mild outside it was really, really warm.

And I was dressed for an Arctic expedition.

The first part of my journey passed off without a hitch. I stealthily made my way through the park by avoiding the paths; I walked as quietly as possible from one tree to another covering open ground but avoiding people. At the War Memorial, I could see the park gates ahead of me and the busy Market Place and High Street beyond.

Breaking cover, I hit the street and was soon through the Market Place. I turned into the High Street, head down and marched onwards.

Nana Grundy says that there are two types of people in the world: those who move out of the way for other people and those who don't. Nana is definitely one of the ones who doesn't and on the Saturday before the Easter weekend, so was I. I walked straight down the middle of the pavement, not looking to my left or to my right, eyes down to the ground, scattering old ladies and children in my wake. It was rude and impolite but needs must when the devil drives (as Nana Grundy is also fond of saying).

Nearly there, nearly there. All I had to do was get to the end of the High Street, cross the road and I'd be a few short steps from Nana and Grandpa's house.

What could possibly go wrong?

Molly Moon, Penny Tupper and Sophie Gallimore (SOPHIE GALLIMORE!) walking around the corner into the High Street at exactly the same moment that I was speedily trying to make my escape from it, that's what.

I think I collided with Penny first, before bouncing off Molly into Sophie. It was difficult to tell the exact sequence with my bobble hat pulled halfway over my eyes.

In any event, I was the one who ended up in a heap on the ground.

'Emmabella? Is that you?' asked Molly.

'Why are you dressed like that?' asked Penny.

'She's hiding her silver bra!' said Sophie.

In a flash, I was back on my feet and on my way like a sprinter out of the blocks. Crossing the road, I could still hear my friends (and Sophie) laughing, as, beneath my disguise, my cheeks burned like hot coals.

I could see sanctuary in the shape of Nana and Grandpa's house ahead of me when I spotted something even more troubling than Molly, Penny and Sophie a little further down the road. Mark

Dangerfield was on Nana and Grandpa's street walking towards me.

Mark Dangerfield! What was he doing here?

Thinking quickly, I checked for traffic and then crossed to the other side of the road.

So did Mark.

What was happening? What was I doing? Why hadn't I thought that he might cross the road, too? Idiot, idiot, idiot.

What now?

I crossed back over the road and shook my head at the same time to indicate that I was confused and didn't know what I was doing (I didn't!). At least Mark wouldn't know it was me beneath my hot and heavy disguise.

As I reached the opposite pavement again, the short path to Nana and Grandpa's house was directly in front of me. I marched up it purposefully and pressed the bell.

'Hi, Emmabella,' Mark called from the other side of the road.

Damn! Damn! Damn!

'Hi, Mark,' I whispered as I continued to jab at the bell.

'Is it cold out?' asked Grandpa Grundy as I followed him through to the kitchen. 'The forecast said it was due to brighten up today.'

'I've got a bit of a sniffle,' I lied, 'so I thought I'd better wrap up.'

I stayed wrapped up to allow my cheeks to return to something approaching their normal colour.

I knew Grandpa would be on his own as it was a Saturday afternoon and Nana would be at her usual poker game. I also knew the thundering advice Nana would have given me had she been there: 'Shoulders back, chin out, *face* them down!' While there was no doubt some merit to this I thought I might get a more sympathetic hearing from Grandpa.

'I bet you're getting it right royally ripped out of you at school,' he said with a chuckle as he turned off the radio.

Or perhaps not.

I quietly got on with making Grandpa a cup of tea and tried to avoid looking at the copy of *The Bugler*, the one with the fateful photo splashed right across the front page, which was sitting on the kitchen table in front of Grandpa.

'Why are you looking so sad?' he asked as I lowered my hood and took off my bobble hat and scarf.

'Because...' I replied, as if that would explain everything.

'It looks bad now,' he said as he held up his copy of *The Bugler*, 'but it probably won't last. This is just tomorrow's fish paper.'

I had no idea what 'fish paper' was but I was more worried about his use of the word 'probably'.

'Probably?' I said.

'Names can stick, unfortunately. When I was at school my mates started calling me 'Pug', I've no idea why. 'Here he comes, Pug Grundy' and the like. I still bump into Stan Smith from time to time; he still calls me Pug.'

I groaned.

'I thought I was going to be famous,' I said.

'And you are,' he said. 'Or rather, you're infamous.'

'That's the bad type of famous, isn't it?'

'Is there a good type of famous? It's a strange world we live in where everyone wants to be famous. Whatever happened to discretion and privacy?'

'I don't know,' I said, because I really didn't know.

'Look, you were trying to do the right thing. You were giving Maisie a hand and you were trying to save the Library. All the rest is flotsam and jetsam.'

'What does that mean?'

'It means it's of no consequence.'

'But it is! I *am* getting it right royally ripped out of me at school. And out of school, too.'

'It'll pass in time. But for now, you're going to have to wait it out. Try to be patient. Your friends at school will soon find something else to get excited about.'

'Do you think so?'

'Of course I do.'

'Have you ever been in the paper, Grandpa?'

'I have not. And nor would I want to be.'

'Why not?'

'Because the first, last and only time that my name appears in that paper will be when my death is announced in the Notices column.'

'Grandpa!'

'It's true. So let's hope it's not for a long time yet.'

I had hoped Grandpa might be able to offer me some words of comfort to cheer me up. It wasn't exactly going to plan.

And then the doorbell rang and my plan went out of the window altogether.

'Who can that be?' asked Grandpa as he eased himself up from the chair.

It was Auntie Maisie. Could this day get any better?

I hadn't seen Auntie Maisie since the disastrous photo had appeared in the paper and from the way in which she breezed into Grandpa's house, it was obvious that she wasn't at all bothered about it.

'Now, Dad,' she said as she came along the hall, 'you must use the Library.'

'I do,' he replied.

'It is most, *most* important that everyone uses the Library. Particularly now.'

'I do use it,' he repeated.

'If people use the Library, actually go there and use it, it'll make it a lot harder for them to close it down.'

She noticed me.

'Oh, hello Emmabella. What are you doing here?'

I wanted to say, 'I'm seeking comfort, support and refuge at Grandpa's because the neatly ordered and arranged life I once knew is now effectively over because I kindly agreed to help you protest against the closure of the Library and the local paper decided to publish a photograph which has made me the subject of ridicule and derision.'

But I didn't say that. I said, 'I just called round to see Grandpa.'

'Well done,' she said. 'And thank you. Thank you for all your help last Saturday. It wouldn't have been the same without you. We'd have been a letter short for one thing and then where would we have been?'

'Spelling out the words, 'Your a Silver Ba',' I said quietly.

'Ha, ha! Yes, of course. You're right.' She turned back to Grandpa, 'So make sure you use the Library.'

'I do use the Library, Maisie, every week. I'm one of the few who do.'

'Good. Carry on using it.'

'I will. Listen, Maisie,' said Grandpa, 'Emmabella's a bit upset about the picture in the paper.'

'Is she?' she turned back to me. 'Are you? Why?'

'Isn't it obvious?' said Grandpa, before I'd had a chance to respond.

'Oh, don't be silly. It's all publicity for our cause.'

It wasn't *my* cause, I thought.

'And there is no such thing as bad publicity.'

Yes, there jolly well is, I thought.

'Without struggle, there can be no success,' Auntie Maisie declared.

Why can't there be success without struggle, I thought. And why I am the only one who is struggling?

'Come on,' said Auntie Maisie, 'I'll give you a lift home.'

I picked up my scarf and bobble hat.

'The world is warming up, Emmabella. Bobble hats and scarves will soon be a thing of the past.'

Not if I keep taking part in your hare-brained schemes they won't, I thought.

At least Auntie Maisie saved me the trouble of having to walk home through the town, thus avoiding any further embarrassing encounters.

Back at home I lay on my bed and tried to read my dictionary. This was usually very enjoyable; I could lose myself in my dictionary for ages. But on that Saturday afternoon, I couldn't concentrate. Something was nagging away in my brain. It wasn't the photo in the newspaper, it was something else. But what?

Of course!

Mark Dangerfield had said 'Hi' to me.

J is for Joke

Take my word for it; you never know when a joke is going to come in handy. So here's a joke just for you.

A balloon boy was born to a balloon mum and balloon dad. When the balloon boy grew older he made friends with balloon boys and balloon girls and together they went to the balloon school where they were taught by balloon teachers. Balloon Boy's balloon parents, his balloon friends and his balloon teachers all thought that he was a very polite and well-behaved boy.

But one day he wasn't.

As he walked to school, Balloon Boy spotted something shiny glinting on the ground. As he got closer he could see that it was a pin. Balloon Boy picked it up and as soon as he got to school he pushed the pin into his balloon best friend's arm. POP! went his friend.

On seeing this, his balloon teacher rushed over to find out what had happened. Balloon Boy popped her, too.

This is fun, thought Balloon Boy. He popped the rest of his balloon friends and then he popped the balloon headmaster and then he popped the school itself.

Looking around, Balloon Boy realised that there was nothing left to pop so he stuck the pin into his own balloon arm and popped himself.

A few days later, the damage had been repaired. All the trouble that he had caused had been put right. Even the pinhole in Balloon Boy's balloon arm had been mended.

Back at school, the balloon headmaster called Balloon Boy into his office.

'You know what you've done, don't you?' the balloon headmaster said, very sternly. 'You've let your teacher down, you've let your friends down, you've let me down and you've let yourself down. In short, Balloon Boy, you've let down the whole school.'

Remember this. You never know when you might need it.

K is for Keel Over

That's what Uncle Dougie did when he slipped on a wet rock as we were nearing the summit of Outerside. His ankle completely gave way beneath him.

For want of anything better to do, I was watching him striding out ahead of me towards the summit and I saw the whole thing. He hit the ground like a felled tree.

'Damn!' he yelled as he lay there on the ground. Actually, he didn't yell 'Damn!' he yelled something far worse but I'm not going to repeat it here.

What is it with my family and ankles? Finn had sprained his ankle sliding down the stairs on a metal tea tray last year, Dad was recovering from his broken ankle and now Uncle Dougie had done something to his. Perhaps some vengeful god or devil had put an ankle-related curse on my whole family. I walked gingerly over to where Uncle Dougie was slumped on the ground, just in case.

As Dougie wasn't screaming in agony as Dad had done on Christmas Eve my initial medical assessment was that his ankle wasn't broken.

'Are you all right?' I asked as I stood over him.

'Of course I'm not bloody all right!'

Sorry…

'Can you stand?' I said, trying to be helpful.

'Not at the moment. I think it's a sprain.'

'As long as it's not broken, ha, ha.'

'There's nothing funny about this.'

'No, of course not. Sorry.'

'I need to get my boot off to see what the damage is.'

'I don't think that's a very good idea,' I said.

'Why?' he said sharply as he began to unlace his boot.

'Well,' I said, 'when Finn sprained his ankle last year it really swelled up. It was huge. If you take your boot off you might not be able to get it back on again.'

After much heaving and grimacing, Dougie, having completely ignored my wise words, finally managed to ease his boot off.

His ankle was massive!

As he tenderly rolled down his thick woollen walking sock I could see that it was also blue! Urghh!

He couldn't get his boot back on again.

Dougie tied the boot to his rucksack with its laces and carefully slid his thick sock back over his swollen ankle. Gently, he eased himself up and on to his good leg and then hopped around on the tufty grass as he tried to establish some degree of balance.

I watched him bounce around wildly for a few minutes before going over to help. I didn't have any choice.

With his arm slung around my shoulder he, at last, managed to get some control over his good leg and he stopped hopping.

Unfortunately, he was now clamped to me. This holiday was getting further and further away from neatly ordered and arranged by the minute.

We looked around. There were no other people to help. There were a few sheep scattered around but they were busy chewing grass and watching the two of us nervously. Who could blame them?

As Dougie leaned into me, he fished his mobile phone out of his pocket. No signal. It was just me and Dougie up a mountain with only three good legs between us.

'I'll have to help you,' I said.

'Just give me a minute, Emmabella. The best thing for a sprain is to walk it off. Let me get my breath back and I'll see if I can put some weight on it.'

Clouds skittered overhead, the sheep wandered off, the weather changed from bright blue skies to low, clinging mist and, after quite some time, Uncle Dougie tried to put some weight on his injured ankle.

He yelled out in agony.

'I think,' he said, after he'd stopped screaming like a hungry baby, 'you are going to have to help me.'

'Happy to,' I lied.

We somehow established a workable system in which Dougie, arm around my shoulder, managed to hop along as I tried to walk at a speed that he could keep up with. For want of a better description, I was Uncle Dougie's crutch.

'We're going the wrong bloody way,' said Dougie, still angry, after we'd taken a few successful steps/hops. 'The path back down to the valley is that way.'

'We're not going down yet,' I replied. 'The summit is up there and we are going to the summit.'

'Leave me here,' he said. 'You go up to the summit and pick me up on the way back.'

'We're *both* going to the summit. You've made it this far and it's just a little further.'

As is the nature of these things, it turned out to be a little bit further than 'just a little bit further' but we got there in the end.

I lowered Uncle Dougie down on to the edge of a large pile of stones that marked the top of Outerside and wandered off a little distance away. I needed some time on my own.

I breathed in deeply. I'd made it! I'd made it to the top of a mountain.

I breathed in again and kept the air in my lungs for as long as I could. The air on top of a mountain must be different, I thought, because it is so far away from the real world below. Mountain air *must* be fresh, clean and uplifting. If anything was going to clear my mind of my Silver Bra worries then this was it.

Sometimes on Boxing Day we'll go for a walk. It doesn't have to be a particularly long walk — we might go down to the river on the edge of town and walk a little away along the bank, something like that. The reason we go is because we'll have spent the whole of Christmas Day inside eating food and playing games and Mum'll say, 'Let's go for a walk to blow the cobwebs away.'

And that was what I was trying to do on Easter Sunday on top of Outerside — I was trying to blow the cobwebs away.

But it wasn't working. I kept breathing in the clean air but the cobwebs, I could tell, were still there.

Sophie Gallimore, my struggles in Mr Coe's creative writing class, King Spider (actually sitting on his *actual* cobweb) and, most of all, the painful Silver Bra episode — they all refused to budge. I knew, right there on that lonely hilltop, that Silver Bra and the rest weren't going anywhere. The giggles, the taunts and teases that I'd gone through before Easter would still be there when I got back to school.

Nothing had changed.

'The weather's starting to close in,' shouted Uncle Dougie from his seat on the ground, 'we should get moving.'

'One more minute,' I replied.

I'd thought I might get a nice view of the surrounding area from the top but there was no hope of that. Huge clouds the colour of the graphite that runs through the middle of a pencil blanketed the valleys below. It was like standing on top of a hardboiled egg that was covered in grey marshmallows.

Even though I couldn't see the surrounding hills I could somehow feel their presence; their weight, their permanence and their scale. It was awe-inspiring and exhilarating and it made me feel small and insignificant which was exactly how I wanted to feel. Being 'significant' and being 'infamous' was horrible. There on that hill, I was an ant; small, almost invisible and easily overlooked. It was bliss.

Perhaps, I thought, I should stay here in the lakes and the mountains where everything is so stunningly lovely that no one would ever notice me. That felt like a good idea. But where would I live? I'd probably have to live in a tent and that wouldn't be lovely at all. Perhaps it wasn't such a good idea.

Easter Sunday was our last full day in the Lake District. On Monday we'd pack the tent into the car and drive home and two weeks after that I'd return to school to discover my fate. The summit of

Outerside was exhilarating but I would have to return to the real world and normality. Except normality wouldn't be the normality I'd always known. Normality would now be a world where everyone called me Silver Bra and it was going to be awful.

I turned around, picked up Uncle Dougie and we set off down the path that would take us back to the valley floor and reality.

L is for Logorrhoea

Logorrhoea, which was one of the mystery words Mr Coe left us to look up at the end of one of his classes, means being excessively talkative. On our walk, Uncle Dougie was definitely not that.

At least not to begin with.

M is for Mistaken

With Uncle Dougie still being quiet (to be fair to him, he did appear to be in some pain and the sock on his bad foot was quite soggy and covered in mud and heather) I tried to cheer myself up by thinking of a good thing.

The very best thing that had happened to me since Christmas was that I had received another Valentine's Day card.

Although reminiscing about this made me feel a bit better I had to admit that the person who I'd hoped had sent me the Valentine's Day card last year was not the same person who had sent me a Valentine's Day card this year.

Allow me to explain.

On the Valentine's Day before last, I received my first ever Valentine's card. I really, really hoped that it had been pushed into my school bag (where I had found it at the end of the school day) by the magnificent Mark Dangerfield. I had sort of cemented this idea in my head and convinced myself that it must be true because the message in the card was a big question mark like this:

?

This, I'd told myself, was not just a punctuation mark; it was also a statement, a statement that said 'Question Mark'; which was, of course, what I wanted to do.

'Mark, do you want to come to the park on Saturday?'

'Mark, shall we go to the school disco together?'

'Mark, the fair's coming to town next week. Shall we go?'

'Mark, how do you get your hair to look so shiny and perfect?'

I could go on.

It goes without saying that between February last year and February this year I hadn't asked Mark any of these questions. I daren't. What if I'd got the wrong end of the stick completely and he hadn't sent the card? That was surely possible.

I'd been thinking over all of this throughout the whole of last year but I hadn't a clue what to do about it. At Christmas, I'd decided that something needed to be done so by the time I'd gone back to school I'd devised a plan of action. Valentine's Day was only a few weeks away and I was determined to confirm one way or another whether it had been Mark who had sent the card.

It wasn't an entirely foolproof plan because it relied on two very important factors:

1) Mark was definitely the person who had given me the first Valentine's Day card.

2) Mark would decide to give me a second card on the following Valentine's Day.

As I say, not foolproof but it was the best that I could come up with.

In short, my plan was to watch Mark like a hawk for the whole of Valentine's Day.

My first idea had been to watch my school bag for the whole day but I quickly realised that that wouldn't work. We'd all be shooed outside at break times so it wouldn't be possible. The next best thing was to spend the day watching Mark. We were in the same classes; we had breaks at the same time and I already spent most of my time watching him anyway. What could possibly go wrong?

In the end, only one thing went wrong…

On Valentine's Day, we trooped into school when the bell went and I hung my bag on the peg outside our form room. I mooched about in the corridor (shoelaces retied – twice) to ensure that I was the very last one into class. Mark was seated at his desk when I went in. Phase one was complete. My bag was on its peg and Mark was in my sights.

I kept my eyes on Mark for the rest of the day (apart from once when he had to go to the loo but that was across from the Science Lab well away from our form room and my bag). In all our classes he was never more than a few desks away from me. At break times I stayed on my own and at a discrete distance from Mark. We were in the same sitting at lunch; he had fish fingers and chips (so did I) followed by syrup sponge and custard (so did I). He *never* left my sight.

The bell went at the end of the day and that's when the thing that I said had gone wrong went wrong. Everybody piled out of the classroom and I kept my eyes firmly locked on Mark. After being so vigilant all day, now was definitely not the time to let my guard down. He walked out of the room, chatting in the lovely way in which he chats to people, pushed his folder into his bag, slung it over his shoulder and was gone.

He didn't go near my school bag. He hadn't been anywhere near my school bag all day.

And yet when I got to my bag to put my own folder away, what did I find nestled inside? You're ahead of me here, aren't you? And you're right. There inside my bag was a Valentine's Day card. The envelope was the same size as the previous year's (I'd kept the envelope as well as the card) and the writing on the front was in the same handwriting, too. It was just my name in thick black magic-marker ink.

It was nice to get another card.

It was heart-breaking to discover that it hadn't come from Mark.

At home, I trudged upstairs and slumped down on my bed. I opened the envelope to find a card that had a picture of a soppy-looking teddy bear clutching a big red heart beneath the words 'Be My Valentine' on the front. Inside, in a slight variation to last year's message, this one had two big question marks, like this:

I tried to resist the urge to speculate on the significance of these marks but I couldn't. Question mark, question mark. Question Mark, *question Mark!*

Ask Mark a question, you silly girl!

But it was no good. I knew the question marks didn't mean what I wanted them to mean because Mark hadn't sent me the card.

How could he have done?

So I'd been mistaken when I'd dared to imagine that Mark Dangerfield had sent me a Valentine's Day card.

I was mistaken when I'd thought that getting down from the top of the mountain would be easy.

I was also mistaken when I'd thought that Uncle Dougie was a miserable so-and-so who had no time for children.

N is for Night

The sky was getting darker and darker; so dark that it felt like night. It wasn't really night, of course – we hadn't been up Outerside that long. But that's how it felt.

I'd thought that climbing up the hill would be the hardest part of the walk. You'd imagine that, wouldn't you? Every step forward is a step upwards, climbing and climbing until the summit is reached. That sounds like the tiring bit, anyway. And it is. But it's nothing in comparison to the return journey. Walking downhill is unbelievably hard. It jars your knees and makes your shins ache with every step. On the very steep bits, your feet feel awkward and wrong because every step is a little bit lower than your feet expect it to be to the extent that every step feels like a surprise. That's how it felt for my feet, anyway.

And for much of the descent I was also trying to support injured Uncle Dougie. He gently slid down the very steep bits on his bottom, trying to hold his injured foot in the air. On the more level parts, he tried, with some resulting pain, to put weight on his bad foot and for the rest of the journey, I tried to help him as much as I could. As far as I knew, Dougie had never had to get down off a mountain with a sprained ankle and I'd certainly never had to help and support such a person.

It was a new experience for both of us.

On the bits where I was helping him, we were, to begin with, completely out of time. Uncle Dougie would hop forward and down on his good foot but he'd fail to coordinate his hops with my steps. After he'd crashed to the ground a few times we both decided that a new approach was needed.

In the end, we came up with a little song which we thought might help our progress (don't get excited, it's not a very good song).

I'd sing, 'One, two, three-step!' and in response, Uncle Dougie would sing 'Hop!' to coincide with my 'Step!' In this way, we managed to develop a good system and we were soon on our way.

'One, two, three-step!'

'Hop!'

'One, two, three-step!'

'Hop!'

'One, two, three-step!'

'Hop!'

O is for Odd

As you can probably imagine, our 'One, two, three-step/hop' song became quite boring quite quickly and I thought Uncle Dougie's enthusiasm for singing was definitely waning. In light of this, I found it really odd when he came up with another song to help us on our way. Obviously made up on the spot, here's what Uncle Dougie started singing:

'I don't know
But I've been told,
When we get down
We'll both be old!'

I laughed.

Not to be outdone in the 'making up rhymes' stakes, I came up with one of my own.

'I don't know
But I've been told,
We'd better rush
Or we'll catch a cold!'

Okay, I know I'm no Sir John Betjeman (and neither is Uncle Dougie) but that's not too bad. And remember, I made it up, off the top of my head, whilst helping an injured middle-aged man down a mountain.

Uncle Dougie found it funny (either that or he was getting delirious) which was also odd. Dougie had never, ever laughed at anything I'd said before.

Soon we fell into a pattern where Dougie would sing a first line and then I'd repeat it and so on with the rest of the little song. And then we'd swap over and I'd make up a new song and sing the first line.

And so the afternoon wore on.

About halfway down the mountain Dougie again tried to walk on his poorly ankle. I watched him grimace and breathe loudly and then fall over.

Helping him up, I said, 'Come on then you abbey-lubber.'

'What does that mean?' he asked.

'It means you're an idle loafer.'

He laughed again (he was definitely delirious), 'Where did you get that from?'

'It's in *Brewer's Dictionary of Phrase and Fable*. I'm reading it at the moment.'

'You're reading a dictionary?'

'Yes.'

'A whole dictionary?'

'Yes.'

'From cover to cover?'

'Yes. It's taking me a while because it's a reference book so I can only read it in the Library.'

'Maisie will be pleased,' he said, shaking his head.

P is for Progress

Through a combination of practice, experience and singing we began to make good progress. This was just as well as the weather was starting to look quite nasty and it was heading down the valley in our direction.

Uncle Dougie was huffing and puffing. I was probably huffing and puffing, too, but his huffing and puffing reminded me of the way he reacted when I'd beaten him at Monopoly on Christmas Day.

'You were determined to win that game of Monopoly, weren't you?'

Weird. Could Uncle Dougie read my mind?

'You always win. I thought that was boring,' I replied.

'It's the way of the world. There are winners and there are losers. The time will come when you'll have to decide which one you are.'

'That doesn't sound like much fun,' I said.

'It's not about fun. It's about success.'

'I'll probably be somewhere in the middle. A winner and a loser.'

'You can tell yourself that, but I think you've got the killer instinct of a winner.'

'What makes you say that?' I asked, surprised.

'That game of Monopoly. I saw the glint in your eye. You were determined to win.'

'That wasn't really me.'

'So why did you do it?' he asked.

'Because I wanted to beat you.'

'I think you've just proved my point.'

We hobbled on, down, down, downwards, down the slope that never ended.

Q is for Question

'Can I ask you a question?' Uncle Dougie said as we continued down the hillside.

'Of course,' I replied.

'What was that all about on top of the hill?'

At the time, on the summit, I think I'd thought that he'd been preoccupied with his ankle and so had not seen me, off in my own little world, trying to clear my mind by deeply breathing in the fresh mountain air. It turned out that he had.

'I was trying to clear my mind,' I said, hoping this would be a satisfactory answer that wouldn't raise further questions. It wasn't.

'What's on your mind?'

I could have put a stop to this by shrugging my shoulders and saying 'Nothing'. But I couldn't shrug my shoulders because Dougie had his arm clasped around them. So instead I said, 'It's the picture in the paper. Everybody's laughing at me. I wish it would all go away but I know it won't.'

'Do you blame Maisie?' he asked.

'No, of course not. It's not her fault.'

'Some people would.'

'I don't.'

Uncle Dougie started laughing. He was laughing at me just like everyone else was laughing at me.

'It's not funny.' I said sternly.

'No, of course not. Sorry.' He went on, 'I wasn't laughing at you; I was laughing at the photo. It's funny.'

'It's funny for everyone else. It's not funny for me.'

'No, I'm sure it's not.'

'Even my so-called friends are calling me Silver Bra.'

He tried to stifle a giggle but he couldn't help himself.

'Sorry,' he said again. 'I'm sure it will all be forgotten when you get back after Easter.'

'But that's the point. I'm terrified of going back to school again and seeing everyone I know. What if I go to join my friends in the playground and they haven't forgotten?'

'Then don't go and join them.'

'But I want to.'

'Then do go and join them!'

'But it's hard!' I yelled.

'Then go and join the other saddos and weirdos who stand in a sorry huddle in the corner!'

The wind was really whipping up now, howling down the valley in a furious rage. But its rage had nothing on me as soon as I realised that Uncle

Dougie had lumped me in with the 'other' saddos and weirdos.

'What?' I shouted above the furious wind that was now swirling around us. 'You think I'm a saddo? You think I'm a weirdo? How dare you say that? I'm the most normal person I know. Ask anybody. Ask Mum, ask Dad. Ask Nana and Grandpa, ask Auntie Maisie. Ask Finn... actually, don't ask Finn. I like normal things, I do normal things. I. AM. NORMAL!'

I paused. I didn't pause because I'd run out of things to say, I paused because I'd run out of breath.

'Anyway,' I continued, lungs now full of air again, 'how do you know there's a bunch of saddos and weirdos who stand in a sorry huddle in the corner?'

Dougie was chuckling now. He was chuckling louder than the wind and he was chuckling at me.

That only made me madder.

'There are saddos and weirdos at every school,' he said eventually. 'There were saddos and weirdos at my school.' He paused for a moment. 'I was one of the saddos.'

'What?'

'I was one of the saddos. I wasn't really a weirdo but I was definitely a saddo.'

'I don't believe you.'

'It's true.'

'But you're so...' I wanted to say 'cocky' but I didn't, '...you're so confident.'

'No, I'm not. Not particularly. It's an act, Emmabella. A front. I'm a successful salesman because I work hard at being a successful salesman. It certainly doesn't come naturally.'

'You're just saying that to make me feel better.'

'No I'm not. Every time I visit a potential client I'm nervous. Very nervous. It's the fear of the unknown. Will they like me? Will they be friendly? Will they be hostile? Will I get an order? No matter how many times I meet new contacts it never gets any easier. I feel the way you'll feel when you walk into the playground after the holiday.'

'So what do you do?'

'I take a deep breath and get on with it.'

'What can I do?' I asked, eagerly.

'You need a triumph,' said Dougie. 'A small triumph to set you back on the right course again. I'm sure you'll think of something.'

I didn't know what he meant but I'd give it some thought. To try to cheer me up, Dougie told me the Balloon Boy joke (See J is for Joke, above). It was quite funny and I laughed so Dougie told me some more jokes.

R is for Recipe

Every single time we go camping, Dad makes his famous Campfire Chilli. It's famous for a variety of reasons – not all of them associated with its taste. I present it here as my Easter 'treat' to you.

Please note, you will not be making this over an actual campfire because campsite owners don't like people making campfires on their land (Mr Cooper who owns the campsite where we stayed in the Lake District definitely doesn't allow campfires. He'd made a sign and everything). So, you'll be making this on a gas camping stove.

To make the chilli you will need:

- Olive oil
- 1 onion (chopped)
- 500g minced beef
- Spice mix
- 1 chilli pepper (chopped)
- 1 can of kidney beans
- 2 tbsp of tomato puree
- 1 mug of water

- Unlimited reserves of patience and determination

Here is exactly how Dad makes his Campfire Chilli:

1. Light your camping stove. When the howling gale you'll no doubt be making this chilli in blows the flame out, light it again.

2. Find the most sheltered place that you can, this might be behind the tent, at the side of the car or up against a dry stone wall, and light the camping stove again. Pray that it stays lit.

3. If it is possible, heat a small amount of oil in a large pan and add the chopped onions. Cook until softened.

4. Add the mince and brown it as well as you can.

5. Add the spice mix. Dad makes his spice mix up before we leave home and then puts it in a little plastic bag. It consists of equal quantities of paprika and chilli powder. How much you add will probably be determined by the strength of the wind at the time.

6. Add the tin of kidney beans. If you can be bothered (and if you've remembered to bring a colander) you can rinse the beans under the communal campsite tap.

7.   Add the tomato puree and the mug of water. Add slightly less than the full mug if it's raining.

8.   Let the whole thing bubble away until the liquid has reduced and it tastes vaguely like chilli con carne.

9.   Try not to let the camping stove blow over. If this happens give up and find the nearest fish and chip shop.

As you make this, do feel free to liberally use the word 'Damn!' with increasing levels of volume and intensity. That's what Dad does.

I should add, in fairness to Dad, that this bears no resemblance to the chilli he makes at home. He makes his 'proper' chilli with stewing steak that he cuts into tiny pieces and it definitely doesn't contain any kidney beans. It cooks very slowly for most of an afternoon and it makes the house smell wonderful.

S is for Subaltern

According to my dictionary, a subaltern is an officer in the British Army below the rank of captain.

It's not quite as interesting as I'd hoped but at least I know.

T is for Ticket Collector

At some point on our never-ending and relentless descent from the summit of Outerside on Easter Sunday, Dougie and I took a break and sat on the damp grass with our backs against a clump of spongy heather. We were both a little bit weary by this stage so I reached into my rucksack and fished out the bar of Kendal Mint Cake that I'd bought in Keswick on Good Friday. Dad had said that it could give you an energy boost and I think that was what we both needed.

I broke off a chunk and passed the bar to Dougie.

I enjoyed the minty flavour but wow! was it sweet. I thought it was going to melt my teeth.

Dougie seemed to enjoy it, though. He polished off most of the bar before handing it back to me. I suppose he was doing a lot of hopping so he probably needed the energy more than I did.

'I used to know this guy – let's call him Peter – who used to get the train to school every day,' said Uncle Dougie.

Where's he going with this? I wondered. 'Did you?' I asked, as brightly as I could manage.

'Lots of the other kids used to walk or cycle to school but Peter lived a few miles away and the easiest way for him to get there was on the train. The morning train always had the same ticket collector who was the most arrogant and mean person you could imagine. He never said "Good morning" and he never said "Thank you". He was rude and surly. He'd go up to each passenger and bark "Ticket!" before strutting off down the carriage.'

'Why was he like that?' I asked.

'I don't know. Perhaps it was the uniform. Give some people a uniform and it goes to their heads. They go off on a power trip. Who knows? But anyway, he was a bully. A bully and a nasty piece of work.

'One Friday morning, Peter was riding the train to school and he was a bit tired, he was probably dozing. So when the ticket collector appeared before him and shouted "Ticket!" Peter was still half asleep. As Peter wasn't quick enough to present his ticket the collector kicked him in the shins and shouted "Didn't you hear me? Ticket!"

'You're kidding?' I said.

'Like I said, he was a bully. Peter thought about that kick for the whole of the weekend. He could let the ticket collector win and forever have one over him or…'

Here, Uncle Dougie paused. 'Or what?' I asked.

'Or he could take his revenge.'

Uncle Dougie's story was getting better by the minute.

'So he came up with a plan,' Uncle Dougie continued. 'On the Monday of the following week, the ticket collector arrived in front of Peter, as usual, and growled, "Ticket!"

'Peter looked straight into the collector's eyes and said, "I haven't got one."

"Then I'll have to throw you off the train," the ticket collector replied with a smirk.

'And it was at that moment that Peter grew as a person and realised that he wasn't going to be pushed around anymore. He'd already had the courage to say he didn't have a ticket but *this* was his moment. This was the moment he'd face the ticket collector down.

"I'd like to see you try," said Peter.

"No ticket, no travel. Get off at the next station."

"No thanks," said Peter, "I think I'll stay on until it's my stop."

"I'll forcibly eject you," said the ticket collector, his face getting redder by the second.

"You can't lay a finger on me," came the reply.

'The ticket collector stormed off and brooded at the end of the carriage.'

'Wow!' I said. 'What happened next?'

'Well,' said Dougie, 'this was a Monday. Peter did the same thing on the Tuesday, the Wednesday and the Thursday. Every day, no ticket. As the week went on the ticket collector got madder and madder. But Friday was different. On Friday, the ticket collector entered the carriage as usual but this time he wasn't alone. He had two police officers with him.'

'No way!' I said. 'Peter's for it.'

'So the ticket collector and the police officers went up to Peter but the collector didn't say a word. He just stood there, arms folded, with a broad and satisfied grin on his face as one of the policemen said, "I think you'd better come with us, son."'

I was really enjoying this. 'What happened then?'

'Peter looked up at the ticket collector and then at the police officers and said very innocently, "Why do I have to do that?"

"Because," the officer replied, "you don't have a valid ticket for this journey."

'Peter's eyes never left the ticket collector's face as he reached into the pocket of his school blazer and pulled out a ticket for that journey on that day.

"Here's my ticket," he said calmly.

'It looked like the ticket collector was about to explode.

"It's a con, it's a trick," the ticket collector yelled. "He hasn't had a valid ticket all week!"

"Is this true?" one of the police officers asked.

'And it was then that Peter provided the perfect icing on his cake of revenge. 'He carefully reached into his blazer pocket again and pulled out four more train tickets. One for every day of that week.'

'*No* way!' I said. 'He'd had a ticket for every single day?'

'He had, yes,' said Dougie, a small smile cracking his usually stony face. 'Do you know what apoplectic means?'

'No – I can look it up when we get home.'

'It means raging, going mad with rage, really. And that's what the ticket collector was. He was apoplectic.'

'What happened then?'

'The train pulled in to *my* station and *I* got off.'

'It was you!'

'Yes, Emmabella, it was me.'

Uncle Dougie had planned and executed a perfect piece of revenge? Unbelievable. Actually, on reflection, it wasn't unbelievable at all. I could all too easily believe it.

'Why Peter? Why didn't you say it was you?'

'I don't know. I said it was someone I used to know and that's the truth. I'm not the same person now that I was back then. We don't just live one life, Emmabella, we all live different lives. The life you are living now is worlds away from the life you'll be living in ten, twenty, thirty years' time. Remember that.'

This is interesting, I thought.

'And also remember,' said Dougie, 'if anyone ever begins a story by saying 'such and such happened to a friend of mine,' or 'I once knew this guy who…' it will almost always be themselves they're talking about. Come on, let's see if we can make it to the bottom of this hill.'

I helped him up and we fell into our, by then, well-practised hopping and stepping routine.

'What happened to the ticket collector?' I asked.

'That's the curious thing,' said Dougie. 'I never saw him again. I don't know what happened to him. He might have got himself transferred to another train but, as I said, I don't know and I've never given it much thought. Let's hope he stopped bullying people, eh?'

As we continued our descent from the summit of Outerside I thought about Uncle Dougie's story. His revenge on the bully was brilliant but I was more interested in what he'd said at the end: we all live different lives. Then, on that windswept, wet and wild hillside, I felt that I was only living one life – a life of Silver Bra shame and embarrassment and all I wanted was to live a different life; a life that didn't involve embarrassment and shame. If it could also be at least a tiny bit neatly ordered and arranged then that would be a bonus, too.

I wasn't sure what Uncle Dougie had meant for me to take away from his 'Ticket Collector' story – if anything. And then it hit me. There on that hill and in that gale, I knew one thing for sure – if I was going to live a different life, *I* was the one who was going to have to make it happen.

U is for Unkempt

Unkempt. Isn't that a wonderful word? I think it might be because it ends with 'mpt' together. I'm sure there can't be many words that end like that. Anyway, according to my dictionary, it means 'dishevelled, ungroomed and slovenly' and that's exactly what Uncle Dougie and I were when we reached the bottom of Outerside.

Our clothes were sodden from the dampness in the air that had accompanied our journey back down the hill – it had been thoroughly 'dreich', as Nana Grundy would say. My boots and walking trousers were caked in mud as were Dougie's single boot and the thick sock that covered his bad foot. I also noticed – with a shudder – that his sock had a big lump of sheep poo stuck to it.

In short, it looked like we'd been dragged through a clarty hole backwards.

At the base of the hill, Uncle Dougie sat on a stile to catch his breath before the walk back to his car. I looked up at the mountain and then over to Dougie as he gingerly rubbed his ankle. One of these two – mountain and man – had made me feel a lot better about my situation and as my eyes settled on Dougie I had a staggering realisation – it wasn't the mountain.

At the car, Dougie took off his remaining walking boot and both of his socks, threw them into the back of the car along with our rucksacks and hopped, barefoot, around to the driver's seat. Soon we were on our way.

V is for Vanished

When we got to the campsite the tent was in its new dry spot but nobody was there. Mum, Dad and Finn had vanished.

'They're probably at the hotel with Maisie,' said Uncle Dougie.

W is for Wince

The hotel that Maisie, Dougie, Nana and Grandpa were staying in was amazing. It was a huge country house made of big solid stones on a small hill above Derwentwater (high enough up to avoid any possibility of flooding).

I was sure that on a clear day the view from the hotel's car park would have been amazing – I could see Derwentwater and the lower slopes of the hills that surrounded it but the summits were still covered in clouds. I knew that Outerside was out there, a little way beyond the lake. It was the first mountain I had ever climbed and it felt good to have reached the top. It felt like an achievement.

'Come on, Emmabella. Let's go and find the others,' Dougie said as he hobbled off in the direction of the hotel's large wooden door.

I watched him as he continued to try to put some weight on his still blue foot. Every attempt was accompanied by a wince and a sharp intake of breath.

I turned back to take one last look at the view. I might not have been able to see Outerside but I knew that I would never, ever forget it.

X is for X-ray

Uncle Dougie didn't need an x-ray on his ankle because it was just a sprain.
In case you were wondering.

Y is for Yomp

Dad and Finn and Nana and Grandpa were in the hotel's bar; Mum must still have been with Auntie Maisie.

'What happened to you?' asked Dad when he saw Dougie hobbling in.

'The perils of climbing a mountain,' said Dougie. 'Emmabella is a trouper. I might not have got back down if it wasn't for her.'

'It was nothing,' I said, flustered.

'What are your plans for this evening?' Dougie asked Dad.

'Well, now that you're back I think we'll head to the campsite. I'm cooking chilli tonight.'

'I think we can do better than that,' said Dougie as he hopped off to the Reception area.

'Did you enjoy your yomp, Emmabella?' asked Grandpa Grundy.

'What's a yomp?'

'It's a walk,' he replied, bluntly.

So I told them all about our day, what had happened to Dougie and how good it felt to have finally climbed a mountain.

'Right,' said Dougie as he tottered in from Reception, 'dinner here tonight. I've checked and they can squeeze us all in. My treat to thank Emmabella for helping me down off the hill.'

My smile must have been a mile wide. There was no reaction from Finn (he'd been strangely quiet ever since I got back) and Dad hadn't looked too happy either. I suppose he'd been set on making his Campfire Chilli but he eventually managed to say, 'Thanks, Dougie. That'd be great.'

Dad and Finn went back to the campsite to get me a change of clothes, Dougie went to check on Maisie and I went to get cleaned up in Nana and Grandpa's bathroom.

Z is for Zero

Zero is precisely the amount of food Auntie Maisie ate at the meal we all had at the posh hotel on Easter Sunday evening.

The restaurant was amazing. It was a huge room filled with antique tables and chairs and the tables were full of people laughing and chatting and having a good time. But the restaurant was mostly amazing for being warm, dry and inside. What a treat.

As we sat at the table reading our menus I saw, out of the corner of my eye, a ghostly apparition entering the restaurant. It was Auntie Maisie. She looked completely washed out and grey, almost as if she'd died and been brought back to life which was appropriate for Easter Sunday, I suppose. Dad went over to help her as Uncle Dougie hopped along behind. Maisie and Dougie's all-expenses-paid trip to the Lake District hadn't quite worked out as they'd planned, I thought.

I was next to Finn who was still being unusually quiet. He sat there stock still with his head bowed down.

'Good day?' I asked him.

He didn't speak.

I tried again. 'Finn? Are you okay?'

'Finn?' It was Nana Grundy from the other side of the table. 'Finn! Tell Emmabella all about your day.'

His head remained bowed over his menu as he mumbled, 'We went to the Pencil Museum. Again.'

Soon, one of the waiters was fussing around our table taking our food orders. As well as trying to decide what I wanted to eat, I was also thinking about the 'other life' I was going to have to try to lead if I was to escape my current doomed predicament. I hoped that if I thought about it hard enough I'd be able, like Dougie and his revenge on the ticket collector, to come up with a foolproof plan to get me out of the mess I was in.

'Emma!' It was Mum and as I looked up from the menu I saw that the waiter was looking at me with his pencil poised over his little notepad.

'I'll have the roast lamb, please,' I replied to the waiter's question that I hadn't really heard. I looked down again at the menu lost in my problems and wracked my brain to try and find a solution.

You know that feeling you get when everyone is looking at you? That's the sensation I had in the restaurant. I slowly looked up from the menu to discover that it was true – everyone was looking at me.

'I think you're a bit young for that, Emmabella,' said Nana Grundy.

'A bit young for what?' I asked, not knowing what she was talking about.

It was Dad's turn to speak. 'Emmabella, you asked for a gin and lime.' He turned to the waiter, 'I think she meant lemonade and lime.'

The waiter nodded, turned on his heels and left. Everybody else was smiling and giggling so I laughed, too.

Finn leaned into me and said, 'Nice try, Sis.'

As we waited for the meals to come out I kept a close eye on Auntie Maisie. She looked awful and she wasn't saying much, either. Every now and then she'd nod or shake her head as the conversation swirled around her but even those small movements seemed to be causing her discomfort. As I watched, her face changed colour from grey to green and her eyes started to look very bloodshot.

And then the waiters brought the food out.

Auntie Maisie had ordered chicken soup - 'I might be able to manage a bit of that' - but as soon as it was placed in front of her she shot up from the table, said, 'I think you'll have to excuse me,' and sprinted off, hand over her mouth, in the direction of the toilets. Oh dear. Mum went to check on her.

My roast lamb was delicious, by the way.

Back at the tent in the dark, tiny hours of the night, I awoke with a start. The mountain climb had not managed to blow the boulder and King Spider out of my mind.

The next morning, as we dismantled the tent (hooray!) and packed all the camping gear into the back of the car, Nana and Grandpa and Maisie and Dougie came over to say goodbye. Maisie was looking much better and Dougie was managing, gently, to walk on his bad foot.

'I've got a present for you two,' Nana Grundy said to me and Finn. 'One each.' She reached into her bag and pulled out two T-shirts, one blue and one red. On the front of each of the T-shirts were the words 'I ♥ the Pencil Museum!' in huge letters.

'Thanks, Nana,' I said.

Finn stayed stony silent.

'Fionton,' said Mum, 'say thank you to Nana Grundy for the lovely present.'

'Thank you Nana Grundy for the lovely present,' he said, robotically.

As Grandpa gave me a big hug I said, 'Grandpa, what day were you born on?'

'Wednesday. Why?'

'No reason,' I replied.

'Well,' that was fun,' said Mum when we were in the car and on our way home.

'Fun?' said Finn. 'I've spent the whole weekend looking at pencils.'

Whatever exhilaration and freedom I'd felt on top of Outerside melted away the moment we turned off the main road. As we got nearer to the centre of town I could see the Abbey looming over everything and heard Dad say, as he always did after we'd been away, 'Here we are, almost home. Down the well-remembered lane.'

The Easter weekend seemed a lifetime away as I walked to school on the first Monday back – exactly two weeks after we'd returned from the Lake District. During those two weeks, I hadn't seen any of my friends because I'd mainly stayed at home, alone in my room. To keep myself busy, I'd tried to draw, I'd made numerous efforts to write a poem on the subject of heroism for Mr Coe's writing class and I'd also sharpened every single pencil I could lay my hands on with my new pencil sharpener.

More than anything, though, I'd been thinking or 'mulling' as Nana Grundy would call it.

I thought about Molly and Penny but mostly I thought about Sophie Gallimore. Was she really so bad? Perhaps I just didn't know her and under the brittle and angry face she presented to the world there was a nice person trying to get out. Maybe that was it. Perhaps I'd done something to make her mean to me? I couldn't think of anything but maybe I had.

As I walked through the park on the fateful morning of the first day back at school, I told myself that whatever happened it wouldn't matter. If everyone called me Silver Bra I'd have to get used to it, no matter how hard it might be. Whatever reaction I got I would still try hard at school and I would put more effort in at Art Club. I would continue to investigate Finn's mysterious map and I was also determined to finish the whole of *Brewer's Dictionary of Phrase and Fable*. I had only got as far as the beginning of the letter C because it was hard to read with lots of big words (words I had to look up in a normal dictionary) and it was also fascinating. The last entry I'd read was:

> **Cap of Fools** (*The*). The chief or foremost fool; one that exceeds all others in folly.
>
> 'Thou art the cap of all the fools alive.'
>
> Shakespeare: *Timon of Athens*, iv.3.

Hmmm.

I stopped outside the Abbey and looked up at its huge square tower. The most important thing I decided to do was to try hard in Mr Coe's creative writing class. I knew I had been given a brilliant opportunity and now was definitely the time to make the most of it. I told myself that it didn't matter who else was in the group and it didn't matter how much easier everyone else found the various tasks we were set. What mattered was how much effort I put in and, come what may, I was determined to try harder.

At the school gate I could see Molly and Penny in their usual spot in the playground. Sophie was with them, of course. I took a deep breath and entered the yard. The problem, as I had come to realise, was that it's your friends who remember things. I knew that any of the other children who only knew me in passing as another face at school would have forgotten all about the embarrassing picture in the paper by then. But my friends? No chance.

During the long walk across the playground, I felt an impending moment of truth bearing down on my shoulders; the closer I got the smaller I felt. If they all called me Emmabella I'd know that the photo was forgotten and that all was well and I would be able to get on with my life. If they called me Silver Bra I knew that I'd be doomed; doomed to forever wander the earth with those two horrible words hanging around my neck. It would never go away.

The closer I got to them the more my legs began to wobble and I could feel my blood rushing through my body to my cheeks. Don't blush, I told myself. *Don't* blush. To stop my mind from literally exploding I thought about the climb up Outerside with Uncle Dougie. That had been good and that had, briefly, taken my mind off all of this. I thought about Dougie and his injured ankle and I smiled to myself. I wasn't smiling at his misfortune – I was smiling because he'd overcome his injury and got back to the valley floor (with some help from me – but he had been brave).

Then I thought about Dougie's Ticket Collector story and I smiled again. And there was something else; one other thing that Dougie had said on Outerside: 'You need a triumph. A small triumph to set you back on the right course again. I'm sure you'll think of something.'

Sophie was the first to see me approaching. She smirked. Too late to back out now.

As I joined them, Sophie opened her mouth to speak, 'Morning, Silv-'

'Hello you three,' I said, quickly. 'Want to hear a joke?'

I decided to dive straight in. Usually, when we met after the holidays it was customary for us to catch up with each other and reaffirm our friendship by undertaking the following exchange:

'All right?'

'Yeah. You?'

'Yeah.'

'Great.'

But that could wait for another day. It was time for some humour.

I told them the Balloon Boy joke.

They all laughed – not *at* me, but *with* me. And then I realised that there was also another laugh coming from behind me. And then a wonderful voice said the most wonderful thing ever, 'Go on then, Emmabella, tell us another one.'

It was Mark Dangerfield.

I did tell them another joke. And another and another. I told them all the jokes that Uncle Dougie had told me on Outerside and no one called me Silver Bra. And then the bell rang and we all trooped in for Assembly.

Miss Christie, our Head Teacher, had some bad news to report. Every term the Parent Teacher Association organises a disco for the pupils – it is the social highlight of our school life. Unfortunately, Miss Christie said that this term's disco had been cancelled due to unforeseen circumstances (aren't all circumstances unforeseen? Whenever I try to foresee circumstances – I'm going to be famous! – it never works out the way I foresee it). It was bad news on the one hand – no disco – but on the other hand it was very, very good news because it was all anybody could talk about for the rest of the day. Molly and Penny were particularly sad because they both loved the disco.

At lunch, we sat together, including Mark, and no one called me Silver Bra then, either. Uncle Dougie's jokes had headed off any potential trouble before school and Miss Christie's bad news Assembly had created an even bigger diversion.

It felt as if the 'Silver Bra' episode had been properly laid to rest. I had no idea if Sophie and I were friends; she is so unpredictable that it is impossible to be sure of anything where she is concerned. I didn't know if I wanted to be friends with her, anyway.

The important thing was that my life seemed to be back to normal and everything was just as I liked it: neatly ordered and arranged. In fact, things were better than normal; things were neatly ordered and arranged with added Mark Dangerfield.

At home that night, I was at my desk trying to come up with something to write for Mr Coe's class when a thought struck me. Before the Outerside adventure I couldn't imagine any situation in which I might have thought this but, anyway, here it is: Uncle Dougie, you are my hero (sorry Grandpa).

When I woke the next day I realised with a start that it was morning and not the middle of the night. I had woken up at the time I liked to wake up and at the time I *used* to wake up before I started dreaming about the boulder and King Spider in his cave.

Truly, things were back to normal.

Refreshed after my first good night's sleep in weeks I put on my dressing gown, sat at my desk and wrote the following masterpiece:

On the Nature of Heroism
By E. E. Murray

What is a hero?
It's someone who helps,
When the world makes you want to
Scream, shout and yelp.

When the clouds start to gather

And dull down your day,
Your hero's a breeze
That blows them away.

When your world's a dark place,
With no hope in sight,
Your hero's a candle
Providing some light.

When you're stuck in the gutter –
Sad and downbeat,
Your hero's the kindly hand
That helps you to your feet.

And when your cares race ahead
And you're lagging after,
Your hero might just be a joke,
Your saviour could be laughter.

There. That should be good enough for Mr Coe.

I had intended to write about Uncle Dougie – my new hero – but I couldn't think of anything that rhymed with 'Dougie'. Perhaps I will rename it: *On the Nature of Heroism* or *An Ode to Uncle Dougie*.

'It is a new day!' I announced as I bounced into the kitchen to join Mum and Finn for breakfast (Dad was away surveying things).

'What?' said Finn, groggily.

'You seem very bright-eyed and bushy-tailed this morning,' said Mum between sips of tea.

'Yes, I do,' I said. 'Today is the second day of my new life.'

'When was the first day?' asked Finn.

'Yesterday.' I said, triumphantly.

'Whatever,' Finn mumbled as he sloped off back upstairs.

'Emma,' said Mum, changing the subject, 'Dad and I have been talking; it's your birthday soon and we wondered if you'd like to have a party.'

'Really?'

'Well, you haven't had a party for a couple of years and Finn has so it's your turn.'

'I'd love to have a party.'

'Good. Give it some thought and let me know what you'd like to do.'

I would give it some thought but I already had an idea about what I'd like to do. It was an idea that would, I was sure, cement my re-established position as a normal person and not a Silver Bra and might, just might, make me the most popular girl in my class.

Emmabella will return in *Emmabella's Birthday Day Alphabet.*

Printed in Great Britain
by Amazon